"I'll let you go
when I'm ready."

Bryden's hold on her wrists was firm.
"You're really quite a wildcat. If we're
going to work together—and we are—
we'll have to get along. And we won't if
you keep losing your temper for no
reason—"

"It wasn't for no reason," Tania shot back.
"You were laughing at me. And you're a
brute, as well. Why don't you go whole
hog and spank me? That's the traditional
way you male chauvinist pigs—"

"Don't tempt me," he said. Suddenly he
released her wrists and put his arms
around her very tightly, bent her head
back and kissed her firmly on the mouth.
For a few moments it was a punishment
for her temper. Then suddenly it wasn't.
It was what Tania had waited for all
her life....

CHAPTER ONE

TANIA heard Ben barking as she neared the lodge gates, and tooted the horn on her Lambretta to let him know she was home. His answering yelp of delight was loud enough to tell her that he was in the run at the back.

She grinned to herself as she switched off the engine and puttered to a halt, leaving the scooter parked by the tree as she went to open the padlock on the enclosed run leading to the kitchen door of the lodge.

'Okay, it's me,' she said, as he went into raptures, hurling himself against the wire netting as if to burst through it. 'Whoa, hold *on*! I'll let you out in a second.'

He hurtled out and straight to a tree while Tania took off her crash helmet and put it on the seat. 'Come on then, walkies,' she told the dog. It was a pleasant, late summer's day, and soon, within a week, it would be the holidays. Six weeks of freedom from noisy eight-year-olds was a prospect Tania looked forward to with unmixed pleasure. They were fine, normally, but the approach of the long summer holiday affected their work. They were exuberant, resistant to schoolwork—— She sighed a little sigh, and smiled to herself as she walked with Ben through the trees, in the direction of the Grange. They weren't bad kids, really, just full of high spirits and energy, but lately she'd been feeling tired. Perhaps I'm ready for this holiday myself, she thought. And maybe I'll think about that holiday with Ted, in Spain.

Then she saw the car, and stopped in her tracks. No

wonder Ben had been barking more noisily than normal! He'd been trying to let her know in the only way he could that someone had been near the lodge house. The Grange was empty, had been for seven years, and now no one came near save inquisitive village children to explore its maze of rooms and corridors or play adventure games in the wilderness of trees that surrounded it. She turned a blind eye, because they did no damage, not since that day she'd given them a talking to in class. The car was a very old, battered-looking Mini, dark blue. Tania called Ben to heel and walked towards it. She wasn't frightened. Living alone at the Lodge since her grandfather died had taught her self-reliance, and she'd always had a strong streak of independence, but at the same time it was very reassuring to have the huge golden labrador at her side. He loped along, tongue hanging out, a few paces in front of her, tail wagging as if to say: 'There, I tried to tell you!'

The car wasn't parked at the front of the Grange, it stood at the back, by the kitchen door, which was open. She didn't like that. Whoever had come, if he—or she, or even they—were on a legitimate errand, surely they would park at the front, outside the magnificent steps? A teeny shiver of apprehension touched her spine. She could go back to the Lodge and telephone the village bobby, George Medley, who would come on his bike straight away. She taught his younger son Robert, and George had always told Tania to call him if she ever needed him. He was a stolid, reassuring policeman whose main hobby was beekeeping, and who liked nothing better than to talk about it. He also kept Tania supplied, via Robert, with delicious honey.

'Don't be silly, she chided herself, and walked slowly towards the open door. Ben's with me....

He followed her in, and it was cool and shadowy in the familiar grey stone passage leading to the kitchen. Tania walked along it very quietly, not quite on tiptoe, but making no sound. The kitchen was empty, dust-covered, dank and cold. All was silent, until a loud thud came from somewhere above, and Ben growled low in his throat, the fur ridging on his spine as he looked at Tania. That was the moment she felt like turning and running. Indecisive, she stood poised for flight, her heart bumping erratically, so loudly that the sound seemed to fill the room.

'Ben,' she whispered, 'come home——' and turned, and as she did she heard the clatter of footsteps on the bare staircase and caught Ben's collar and held him, ready to pull him out. There was still time——

Then there wasn't time, because a man appeared in the doorway, and Ben tried to lunge forward. Tania hung on to his collar for grim death, and the man said, in a deep voice:

'What's this? A welcome committee?' She couldn't see him properly because he was standing in the shadows where the light didn't reach, but she could see enough to know he was very big, very tough—and very gipsyish-looking. A tinker! She should have known, by that disgusting car outside. They came round every so often, buying and selling scrap metal and just about anything else they could, and some were a menace. He wouldn't be alone, that was the disturbing thing. She wanted to get away, out into the open air. Her house was empty, her Lambretta left for anyone to steal....

'Come on, Ben,' she said, and pulled at his collar, but

ineffectually. Ben wasn't budging. Ben was staring at the man, his body quivering.

'Not answering?' The man laughed and walked forward, so that now he was in the room, only feet away. She didn't like his laugh and she didn't like *him* and she wanted to get out, because she knew that some of them carried knives, and she didn't want Ben hurt. He was even bigger, close to, wearing old jeans and checked shirt with sleeves rolled up to the elbow, and a dark tanned face that was somehow vaguely familiar, and black thick hair. His arms were powerful. He looked as though he was capable of knocking someone out with one blow—he looked as though nothing frightened him, not even the strong dog she held. 'Who are you?' he asked.

Tania found her voice. She had wondered if she'd speak ever again. 'Never mind who I am,' she retorted. 'Who are *you*?'

'A visitor to the Grange.' He grinned at her, showing white teeth, mocking her. 'And I'll bet you live at the Lodge?' He laughed. 'I called there on my way in. Your dog nearly went mad, but I talked to him—you can let him go.'

'He'll kill you if I do,' she said, in her most confident tone, more to give herself courage than to convince him. 'That's why I'm going—and I advise you to go too, and your friends——'

'I'm alone,' he cut in. 'There now, that's a relief to you, isn't it? Let him go. I won't harm him.'

'He might harm *you*,' she retorted. He could be speaking the truth. She had heard no more sounds from above, and she was nearer the back door than he, and she could run fast, and so could Ben, if she called him——

'He won't, you'll see.' He moved slightly. 'Hello, Ben, we meet again, don't we?' His voice had gone quieter, softer, and Ben, idiot Ben, who should have known better, whined softly and began to wag his tail as if the man were an old friend, which he most certainly was not. The man held out his hand, walked forward, leaned down, and stroked the labrador's head.

'Good dog,' he said. It seemed pointless for Tania to continue holding her traitorous dog. He hardly constituted a threat—especially not to this confident man. She let go of his collar and Ben leapt up. He was a big dog, but his paws barely came above the man's waist. He continued stroking Ben as he asked: 'Did you think you'd discovered a burglar?'

Tania moved away. She didn't like standing too near to him, yet she didn't know why. 'Not at all,' she said with dignity. 'There's scarcely anything worth stealing. Why are you here?'

He shrugged. 'It's an interesting place. I like interesting old houses. I like *this* house. I might just stay here a while.'

'Here?' She laughed. 'Don't be ridiculous! You can't just walk into a strange house that doesn't belong to you and decide you'll stay!'

'Can't I?' He smiled, a crooked, very amused smile. 'But I just did. So what are you going to do about it?'

Tania's temper was rising rapidly. Already on a short fuse, because of the shocks, she felt her face flame into colour. She took a deep breath. 'You'll see what I'll do,' she retorted. 'Come along, Ben.' Ben didn't move. He ignored her completely in fact, which did nothing to improve her temper. The man pushed him gently down.

'I think your mistress wants you,' he remarked, and

the laughter in his voice was barely concealed.

Tania walked towards the door, followed, reluctantly, by Ben. 'I'm going to get the police,' she said. It sounded better than policeman.

'You mean the village bobby?' he enquired, following her towards the door. 'He'll have to come up on his bike, won't he? That should take him—let me see—oh, fifteen minutes? Okay, I'll be here.'

Tania turned slowly. 'How did you know that?' she demanded.

'Know what?'

'That he rides a bike.'

'Because I called in at the police house to ask directions to this place, that's why, Miss Dean.'

She froze. How did he know her name? 'Why did you ask me who I was if you already knew?' she said icily.

'He—Sergeant Medley, that is—told me.'

She relaxed fractionally. A tinker searching for pickings would hardly call on the police first. At least he wasn't dangerous, that was something. Not much, but something. She stood very tall and straight, and faced him. 'Why?' she demanded.

'Why what?'

'Oh, don't always answer a question with a question!' she snapped.

'Temper!' he said mildly. 'You should make your questions more clear. I mean, is it—why did I call on the policeman, or why did I get your name, or why am I here?'

She wanted to know all three, but she wouldn't give him the satisfaction.

'Why are you here?' she said. In a minute, if he wasn't

careful, she was going to hit him, and hard. Her eyes blazed into his.

'I told you, I like it here.'

'You can't have seen it from the road if you had to ask directions,' she said, 'so you must have known about it before.'

'Oh, very true,' he agreed, bowing his head in mocking acknowledgement of her astuteness. 'Ten out of ten for observation.'

'Don't be so flippant!' she snapped, temper nearly at danger point. He laughed, then moved slightly back as he saw what was there in her eyes.

'Wow, that's one hell of a temper you've got, Miss Dean! Surely a *schoolteacher* should be more calm?'

She didn't care any more. She advanced on him and stood in front of him, arms akimbo, breast heaving. 'How *dare* you!' she stormed. 'How dare you spy on me——'

'I didn't.' He cut her off neatly. 'He told me. Said you taught his youngest boy——'

'I'm surprised he told you anything at all, looking at you—I'm surprised he didn't arrest you straight away——'

'No insults, please,' the man begged. 'You'll make me laugh, and then you'll explode, because you're nearly doing it now and quite frankly, with red hair like that I'm not surprised—I mean, a temper like yours goes with flaming hair. What do the kids call you? Carrots?'

Tania swung out at him, but he blocked her flying arm, caught it, and held it. 'Ah, ah,' he chided. 'Naughty! Now calm down, carrot-top, because there's no way you're going to slap me——'

'Let go of my arm!' she whispered, shaking. 'You're insufferable—you—you——'

He drew in his breath sharply. 'Careful! Language. Don't shock Ben——'

'Damn Ben! Damn you!' She tried to pull her arm free, but he held it, strong fingers encircling her slender wrist.

'I'll let you go when you've calmed down,' he said. 'Now take a deep breath and count to ten. One, two, three——'

'Oh, go to hell!' She lashed out with her left hand, and that too was caught and held. Then he pulled her towards him, slowly, inexorably, until she was only inches away; looked down at her.

'Now what am I to do with you?' he mused. 'Sergeant Medley didn't warn me you were dangerous. He seemed to have quite a high opinion of you, as a matter of fact.' He smiled his lopsided smile. 'It should be interesting, having you as a neighbour.' He moved his hands together, so that then he held both her wrists in one large hand, and with his free one touched her hair, the soft silkiness of it. 'It is real!' he exclaimed as if in surprise. 'Beautiful. Suits you exactly.' Then he tapped her nose. 'Ginger Dean —suits you.'

'It's not Ginger!' she raged. 'It's Tania. T-A-N-I-A— Tania.'

'Ah, now I know. He didn't tell me, you see, just called you Miss Dean. I—er—imagined someone older, quite frankly. Nice name, Tania. Russian?'

'No.' She wasn't about to give him her family history.

'Oh.' He raised one eyebrow in gentle surprise. 'Don't want to talk about it? Never mind. Don't you want to know my name?'

'No! Let me go—you're hurting me!' He wasn't. His grasp was quite gentle. Extremely powerful, but gentle.

'It's Bryden Kane.'

She glared stonily at him. 'I said I didn't want to know your name. I don't *care* what your name is, I just want you to go.'

'And I'm extremely good at making things——'

'Like trouble?' she enquired sweetly, breathlessly. He was *too* near.

'Ha ha, funny joke. No, like window frames, cupboards, repairing things. This place is a wreck——'

'I thought you said you liked it?'

'I do. It's a challenge.'

'You're crazy! You're going to squat here and repair it? For what? It'll be sold and you'll be out, and serve you right. In fact, when I get out of here—*when* you stop playing Superman and let me go—you'll be out so fast you won't have time to sneeze, let alone repair it.'

'You reckon?' He released her. 'Okay, off you go. Phone your policeman. Bring him back here—I'll have the kettle on. Bye-bye, Miss Busybody.'

She turned away and stalked out stiff-legged, praying Ben would follow, yet not daring to look back lest it spoil her exit.

She had reached the path before she heard Ben thundering up behind her, and she glared at him. 'Huh! Fine guard dog you are,' she remarked. Ben looked apologetically at her and lowered his head, lolloping along at a more sedate pace, as if to make amends.

Tania went into her house and picked up the telephone and dialled the police house number. She was still seething from the cavalier treatment at the hands of that man. He'd played with her, treated her like a silly child——

'Hello? Sergeant Medley? It's Tania Dean, there's been

something rather odd at the Grange,' she burst out in a rush.

The policeman's voice came over the line, slow, reassuring. She could almost see him getting his pen, pulling his note pad nearer the telephone. 'Hello, Miss Dean. It's Mr Kane, is it? He's arrived, then? Pleasant fellow. What seems to be the trouble?'

Tania was stunned. Pleasant fellow? Were they talking about the same Mr Kane? *Could* there be two?

'Well, I—er—he—er—seems to intend to *stay*, and it——' she was stammering now. This was ridiculous. She cleared her throat. 'He seems to think it's all right to move in, Sergeant. I mean, people can't just do that, can they?'

'Ah well, you see, Miss Dean, that's correct. Normally not, but you see, he showed me the note.'

'The note?' For a moment a large pound note was conjured up in her imagination. 'What kind of note?'

'From the late Colonel Marchbank's solicitors. Giving him authority to live there while carrying out essential repairs.'

Tania's heart sank. 'You mean——' she squeaked, then took a deep breath. 'You mean he's a *right* to be there?'

'Aye. All legal it was. On proper notepaper, very posh.'

'Oh, I see.' He'd not told her. He'd led her on deliberately. He knew all along, he knew, and he'd toyed with her. 'Right, thank you, Sergeant Medley. That seems to clear it up. Goodbye.'

'Goodbye, Miss Dean. Nice to talk to you.' The phone clicked, and she put the receiver down. He was going to work there. Not to squat, not to steal, but to live.

'Damn you!' she muttered. She went into her kitchen to make a much-needed cup of tea, and looked out of the window at her small patch of garden, enclosed totally by the wire netting of Ben's compound so that he wasn't locked in the house all day. Outside, the trees and luxuriant woods bordering the Grange. And it wouldn't be the same, not now, not any more. Not with a stranger here. She didn't like him, she certainly didn't trust him, but there seemed nothing could be done.

Her kitchen was all bright yellows and browns, cheerful colours, with a row of plants on the windowsill and flowered curtains at the window, and a small breakfast table with yellow formica top and matching stools. Tania enjoyed eating out here. She liked her house. It was small, three tiny bedrooms and minuscule bathroom, and a fairly large lounge which housed her books and television, and, in winter, a log fire roaring up the chimney. Ted liked the Lodge. He often said, jokingly, that he wouldn't mind living in it when they were married, instead of the house his father was building for them. Tania smiled to herself. She hadn't said she would marry Ted, but his father was already building their wedding present, because he couldn't imagine any girl in Granchester not wanting to marry his only son. He thought Tania was playing hard to get. This had been relayed to Tania by Ted in one of his franker moments, and she had laughed, but inside she had known exactly what Jack Latham meant. He really meant that Tania should consider herself lucky to be asked, she who was virtually penniless, living on her teacher's salary in her late grandfather's cottage.

She filled the teapot, seeing again Mr Latham's face, last time they had met at the Lathams' superb detached mansion the other side of Granchester. A bluff, self-made man, he rarely minced words, and he hadn't then. He had stood, one elbow on the elegant Adam mantelpiece, looking down at Tania on the chair. The two of them were briefly alone, Ted having gone to take a telephone call, Mrs Latham supervising the dinner arrangements.

'Well, lass,' he'd said, 'I admire independence in anybody—always been independent meself, so I should know. But don't take it too far. Ted wants to marry you, and I'm building a house you'll not be ashamed to invite the Queen to—so why the stubbornness?'

Tania had smiled. 'I don't believe in rushing into anything. Marriage is for life, and I've only known Ted for six months.'

'But you're the lass he's chosen.' He spoke as if that was it. *She* was chosen. *She* should be grateful. She liked Ted, but she didn't love him. And there was no way you could explain that to a man like Jack Latham who rode roughshod over all opposition to get what *he* wanted.

'I'm very fond of Ted,' she had said.

'Is that all?'

'Yes. He knows. He's patient.'

'But I'm not. He's nearly thirty——'

'And I'm twenty-four, I know.' She smiled at her would-be prospective father-in-law, to soften her words. He spoke as if thirty was the end of the road.

'Aye, you are. Do you know how old Ted's mother was when I married her? Nineteen.'

Yes, she thought, and look at her now. A pale shadow of a woman, who's so terrified of you she looks to you for permission to speak—and you don't *care*. But she said nothing of this, not because it would be unforgivable, but because it would do more harm than good.

'Perhaps,' she said softly, 'you'd prefer Ted to marry a girl of nineteen as well?' She had looked at him, held his hard gaze, and smiled. She wasn't frightened of him like everyone else was, and he knew it, and he didn't like it, but Tania didn't mind. If she married Ted—if— her father-in-law would never dominate her like he did everyone else—even his son. She sometimes wondered if that was one reason she didn't love Ted....

Her thoughts were interrupted by a sound at the back gate in the fence, a rattling, then a man's voice, and Ben's answering bark.

'Anyone at home?' called Bryden Kane, as he tapped on the door.

Tania put her cup down. 'No. Go away!'

She heard him laugh. Then: 'I've come to borrow a drop of milk. May I come in?'

'Will you take any notice if I say no?' She went over to the door and flung it open and glared at him. 'Very funny, Mr Kane. *Very* amusing. You had your little joke at my expense—ha ha, let's all laugh. Pretending to be a squatter when all the time you'd got a note——'

'Ah! You phoned the worthy officer, then?'

'You know damned well I did! Serve you right if I refused to give you any milk——'

'Ah, but you wouldn't, would you?' He leaned on the doorpost and looked down at her, and smiled. 'You wouldn't turn a thirsty man away? Hmm?' He peered over her shoulder. 'Tea? You made some. Lovely. I'm a—er—bit short of that as well, actually.'

Tania took a deep breath. He was going to hear a few home truths. 'You'd better come in,' she said.

CHAPTER TWO

'Nice kitchen,' he remarked as he walked in and looked round. He seemed to fill the kitchen. Tania had not seen him really clearly before in the Grange kitchen, because it was dark and shadowy with the overgrown laurels tapping at the windows. Now, in her bright sunny kitchen, he was perfectly clear. He still looked dark and dangerous in spite of his manner, but the dishevelled jeans and shirt were clean, as was he. His hair really was jet black, and his face was strong and lean, with square firm chin, deeply cleft, wide well-shaped mouth, straight almost classical nose and startling blue eyes. One thick dark eyebrow was lifted quizzically, amused, as he regarded her. 'Seen enough?' he enquired.

Tania looked away. 'You'd better sit down,' she said coolly. 'I'll pour you a cup of tea.' She stalked over to the cupboard for another beaker.

'Thanks. Is the rest of the cottage as nice as this?'

'Yes,' she said shortly. 'Sugar?'

'No, thanks. But you're not going to invite me to see it?'

'How did you guess?' she said sweetly.

He laughed. He was always laughing, damn him, as if everything she said amused him; as if *she* amused him. 'Suit yourself. Thanks.' He took the beaker and drank some tea. 'Nice. I was thirsty—needed this.'

'There are shops in the village,' she pointed out. 'They're open until six.' She looked pointedly at her kitchen clock which showed four-fifteen.

'Then I must go. There's no electricity yet at the Grange. It'll take a few days to have that seen to, and it's very damp, and there's no water——'

'I thought you said you'd have the kettle on!' she said triumphantly, as if catching him out in a lie.

'I hadn't tried it then. When I did all I got was a rattling and moaning. So I've a proposition for you, Miss Dean.'

Tania sat down at the opposite side of the table, her brain working overtime. But what she was thinking was too absurd for words.

'It's this,' he continued after a few moments, as though he had allowed her time to think. As though he knew what was going through her mind, and was letting it sink in. 'How would you like a lodger?'

It was her turn to laugh. 'You've got to be joking!'

'I'm very serious.' He looked at her, and his eyes were very cool, very level upon her, vivid and deep blue, and as strong as the rest of him. 'I need somewhere to sleep, that's all, for a few weeks or so until the essential supplies are working again at the Grange. I shall be there every day until late, and I shall be up early in the morning. You wouldn't even notice me. And I'd pay you twenty pounds a week.'

Twenty pounds for a bed! Tania shook her head. If he'd said a hundred she would still have said no. Didn't he realise how absurd, how totally ridiculous the whole arrangement would be? 'No, I'm sorry,' she said, 'but I wouldn't consider it. I'll let you have water until you get the supply on, but—no, definitely not.'

'I'm sorry too.' He didn't look it, that was the trouble. He was still regarding her with that cool level gaze, and she stirred uneasily. 'Because it leads me to something I didn't really want to have to say. However,' and he shrugged.

Tania's heart beat faster. He didn't know. He couldn't know—she felt very small and afraid, all of a sudden. Her first instinct about him had been right: he was a threat to her and to her safety. She waited for him to speak, and her mouth had gone dry.

'Your grandfather lived here before, didn't he? And he worked on the estate for Colonel Marchbank for many years, and in return had this place rent free.'

She didn't say anything. She couldn't—but she knew now what was coming.

'And it didn't legally belong to your grandfather—and it doesn't legally belong to you——'

'There was a gentleman's agreement,' she burst out. 'What are you trying to say?'

'I'm not *trying* to say anything, I'm telling you. You don't have the deeds, because I've seen them in the solicitor's office. And I am authorised to work here until such time as the Grange is restored to its former glory, and——'

She stood up, too agitated to remain sitting. 'You're trying to get me out!' she exclaimed. 'Did *he* put you up to it? Is it something to do with Latham?'

He looked puzzled. 'Who?'

'Jack Latham—he knew the Colonel. It would just be the sort of trick he'd do——'

'Hold on! No one is trying to get you out—certainly not me. Who is Jack Latham?'

Tania glared at him, not sure whether he was lying. If he was, he was doing it superbly well. 'Look,' she snapped, 'don't lie to me. Everyone knows Jack Latham——'

'I'd appreciate your telling me.'

'He's a builder. The biggest in the country, practically. He knew the Colonel well——'

'Wait a minute. Is he County Construction?'

'You do know! You were lying! So it is him!' She was hurt and angry, and shaking with it. 'Oh God, he couldn't have chosen a better way——'

'Listen.' Bryden Kane stood up and came round to her. 'He has nothing to do with me. Whether you believe me or not, it's the truth. And I am *not* trying to get you out. This place is yours, as far as I'm concerned.'

'But you want to live here?' She stared at him, her eyes tear-filled with impotent rage.

'No, not exactly.' His voice softened. 'Only lodge in your spare bedroom for a brief time—and you'll not even notice I'm here——'

'D-don't be ridiculous! I could hardly n-not notice someone like you. You *had* heard of him.'

'Yes—of his firm anyway. Why does he frighten you so?'

He doesn't frighten me as much as you do, she wanted to retort. But she didn't, because this man, whoever he was, knew too much already. 'I'm going out with his son. He's a very dominant man. He wants me to marry Ted—his son—and he's building us a house. He—it would be just his kind of trick to get me out of here so that I'd be more easily persuaded——'

'Charming man,' he observed.

'You're not doing so badly yourself!' she retorted, some of her fighting spirit returning. She didn't give in easily.

'And you want to marry this Ted?' he went on, ignoring her comment.

'That's none of your business!'

'Is he like his father?'

'That's nothing to do with you!'

'Because, if he is, I wouldn't touch him with a barge-pole.'

'Nobody's asked you. You've nothing to do with my life.'

'Unless I move in.'

'You don't do so badly in the blackmail business either,' she snapped. 'I'm not entirely stupid. If I don't let you stay here I'm quite aware of the implications——'

'Really? And what are they?'

She turned away. 'Oh, go to hell, you make me——'

He caught her and swung her round.

'Can't you answer?' he was holding her, not urgently, but he wanted a reply.

'It's obvious, isn't it? Your friends the solicitors—the Colonel's solicitors—will find some way to get me out——'

'I've said not—in fact I'll guarantee it. But I do need a room.'

How could he guarantee anything? Yet his words had the ring of truth about them. And Tania had no choice. Bryden Kane's hands upon her arms were warm and strong, and she found herself, irresistibly, looking up into those fascinating eyes. She didn't like him one bit, but she couldn't deny that he was magnetic physically. The skin on her arms tingled at his touch.

She ran her tongue over her dry lips. 'I don't have much option,' she said quietly. 'You'd better go and get your things. Tell me—just one question—is the Grange going to be sold when you've done it up?'

'No. I'm not doing it up personally either. There's work

there for a team of men for several months—I shall be supervising. And when it's finished someone will move in.'

'Who?'

'A relative of the late Colonel's. Someone who won't mind you living here as long as you want to. Someone who doesn't want or need this lodge.'

'How do you know?'

'I do, that's all. I'll go and fetch my luggage. It's already in the car outside.'

Tania felt herself go cold all over, just as if someone had covered her in icy water. 'You knew,' she whispered. 'You knew all along that you'd be coming here?'

'Yes. I know a lot of things, Tania.' His eyes were deep-set, hypnotic, mysterious, frightening. They held hers, and she couldn't look away.

'Who—who are you?' she whispered.

'I've told you. Bryden Kane——'

'No, not your name—you. Where do you come from?'

'London. And other places. I'm a wanderer—can't you tell?' His tone belied his serious eyes. 'I roam the world, and I go where I will—and no one stops me.'

'Then why—here? Why come and work here?' She couldn't look away, or move, nor did she want to. His words were having the oddest effect on her, almost as if they were inevitable, and as if she knew what they would be, but had to hear.

'Because there comes a time when the wandering has to stop. I've never been in one place for long enough to see what life's about. Here, when I saw this place, the town nearby, the village—the Grange— I knew that for a while I was going to stay.'

'Your work—is this what you do all over the place? Renovating houses?'

'No. I've done everything—jack of all trades, master of none. So this will be a challenge to me.'

Tania began to shiver. Two hours previously her life had seemed so safe and secure, and normal. And suddenly everything was changed. She was no longer sure of anyone or anything—least of all him. 'How do I know —I'll be safe with you here?' she asked.

'You'll be as safe as you want to be.'

'What kind of an answer is that?' she whispered. The shivering grew to a trembling. Dear lord, what did he mean?

'I don't hurt women—not in any way, Tania. Are you and Ted lovers?'

She felt the treacherous colour suffuse her face. 'No!' she gasped. 'How dare you——'

'I dare.' She had forgotten about Ted for the past few minutes. To say he wouldn't be happy with the arrangements would be the understatement of the year. He'd be furious.

'He won't like this,' she said.

'I'm not staying with him. There's not much he can do about it—except of course to persuade you to marry him. Are you going to?'

'Let me go, please,' she said, and he did. 'I've told you it's——'

'None of my business. Yes, I know. I don't think you are, if you want my opinion——'

'I don't——' she began, and he continued as if she hadn't spoken:

'Because for a start it's quite obvious you don't love him——'

'How dare you! You come marching in here as if you own the place, settling yourself in—that's bad enough—but to make it worse you now start telling me about my private life——'

'I told you, I'm a wanderer, a rover. I like life, I like seeing what makes people tick, what makes them behave the way they do. Don't you? Aren't you interested in life? Or are you content to teach, come home here, walk the dog, go out with what's-his-name——'

'Ted!' she snapped. 'You know very well!'

'I've already formed a picture of what he's like. Do you want to hear it?'

'No.'

'Well, I'll tell you. Fairly tall, about five ten or eleven—fair hair, slim build—weak mouth and chin——'

'He's not!' she burst out indignantly, 'he's good-looking——' She faltered. Damn the man! Why did he have to say that? He was too accurate for comfort, that was the awful thing. But how on earth——

'Probably enjoys tennis and other games that aren't *too* energetic—I bet he's never played rugger.'

'And you have, I suppose!' she snapped.

'Often. It's a man's game.'

'Big deal!' She turned away. 'Just because you're built like a barn door——'

His laughter stopped her and she whirled back, furious. 'Don't laugh at me!' Her temper was coming to the fore again, now that the first fright of eviction had vanished.

'Don't say such funny things then. Barn door! What the hell does that mean? Just because I'm not weedy like him——'

'He is not weedy! He's slim——'

'And I'm not? Thank God I'm not. Don't you like a

man to look like a man?'

'I wasn't aware we were talking about *you*,' she retorted. 'Although you can't stay out of it for long, can
you?' She glared at him, looked him up and down, then
wished she hadn't. He was a perfect physical specimen—
and he very probably knew it, and she wished she could
laugh at him, but the laughter died in her throat, because,
whatever she thought about him, there was no denying
the obvious fact that Bryden Kane was one hell of a man.
'Huh!' she added, for good measure, injecting all the
scorn into it that she could.

'Life with you could be interesting, Ginger,' he drawled.
And, before she could open her mouth to retort, he
added: 'I'll go and get my stuff. Back way or front?'

She swallowed, took a deep breath. What was the use?
He had an answer to everything. 'I'll take you out the
front,' she said. 'Then I'll show you your room. This
way.' She opened the door into the hall and he followed
her. The hall was narrow, with the lounge leading off,
and the staircase curving up at one side. He looked up
and around.

'Mmm, very nice. All compact. Did you decorate this?'

'Yes.' Tania opened the front door. There was a tiny
front garden, filled with rose bushes and shrubs, and a
patch of lawn. Bryden Kane's disreputable car was
parked outside it.

'Excuse me.' He brushed past her and went out, and
she stood watching, arms folded. It wasn't too late. She
could say, I've changed my mind—or could she? She
knew she didn't want to find out.

He lifted out two large suitcases, and she felt a slight
sense of shock at seeing them. Something didn't tie up
here. The car and his own dress were matching, casual

almost to the point of not caring. But the suitcases didn't follow the pattern. They were old, certainly, but it needed only one brief glance to see that they were of expensive hide, much travelled, but honourably shabby with that perpetual air of dignity that is the mark of true quality.

They were loaded too. As he walked towards her carrying them, she could see that. She turned and went up the stairs, leaving him to follow as best he could.

She opened the door to the back bedroom, the smallest, with scarcely room for the wardrobe and tiny chest of drawers it held. He came in and put the cases down. 'Fine,' he said. 'Just fine.' He'd probably have said that if she'd shown him into a cupboard.

'Let's get one thing straight, Mr Kane,' she said. 'There's only one bathroom, and it's there,' she pointed to the door opposite his. 'I hope you have a dressing gown—I mean——' she floundered under his amused gaze. 'I don't want——'

'You paint a perfectly clear picture. No, I don't actually, but fear not, I will buy one tomorrow. Oh, here's your first week's rent.' He took out a twenty-pound note from his pocket and handed it to her. 'I've brought my own towels. May I have a wash after I've unpacked?'

'Of course. I'll be downstairs.' She fled. Safely in the kitchen again with Ben she could hear the sounds as Bryden Kane moved around upstairs. Then the bathroom door closed. She began to prepare her tea. She had bought salad on the way home, and there was enough for two, so it seemed churlish not to make one for him as well, although he would have to make his own arrangements after today, that was definite. She was not going to wait on him. She looked at Ben, who sat, head cocked to one side, listening to the new sounds from above.

'What have I got myself into?' she asked, and Ben wagged his tail as if he understood perfectly, which he might well have done for all she knew. And she still had to tell Ted. That was going to be difficult, she had no illusions about that. Just how difficult, she was fortunately not able at that moment to guess.

'I've made salad for you, Mr Kane——'

'Bryden,' he said. 'Have you? How very kind of you.' He looked at it, set out on the table, and sat down. He had changed his shirt for a plain blue short-sleeved one, and Tania found it difficult not to look at those arms. They were very muscular, and covered with fine dark hairs, not excessively so, but just enough, and he looked terribly strong. Perhaps he had always worked with his hands. She could imagine him being quite at home building a road, or a motorway, or a house.

'Coffee or tea?' she said, managing to look away at last, before he noticed.

'Whichever you're having.' He looked up and grinned. 'Are you going out tonight?'

'No. I've got some lessons to prepare for tomorrow. What will you be doing?'

'I'll go back to the Grange when I've had this, just to finish looking round and seeing what needs doing. Tomorrow I've got to start finding workmen.'

'From round here? You'll have a job.' She felt almost pleased, saying that.

He cocked an eyebrow. 'Will I? Don't tell me they all work for lover boy's father?'

'If you mean Mr Latham,' she said coolly, 'you're almost right. Yes, most of them do.'

'Hmm. Thanks for telling me.'

'A pleasure.' She poured out his coffee and handed it to him. 'Tell me, what are you going to do about food? This first meal's on the house by the way, but you can appreciate I have enough to do without——'

'I was going to ask you that later,' he cut in, and gave her a winning, boyish smile. 'How about another ten pounds for breakfast and evening meal?'

'No, I couldn't.' She shook her head. 'Sorry. It's too much of a dash in the mornings. I only have toast and tea——'

'If *I* did it? I get up early. Don't you?'

'I get up at eight, but I have to leave at eight-thirty——'

'Good, that's breakfast sorted out. I'll have it ready for you at eight precisely. Two pieces of toast, is it? And marmalade?'

'I don't think you understand,' she said weakly. Her resistance was crumbling. She had the most awful difficulty in getting up at all in the mornings and sometimes was only saved by Ben coming up and barking at her, as if he knew. 'It's not that. I—in the evenings I sometimes go out, and I like to have a snack when I get in from school——'

'Yes, but they break up next week, don't they?'

'Well yes, but——'

'That's settled, then. We'll organise a time to suit us both. I'll get breakfast. I can get up at seven and take Ben out if you like. And if you don't want an evening meal I'll get my own. Quite simple.'

'Look, Mr K—Bryden—you can't organise my life for me like this! You've only been here five minutes and already you're trying to take over. I don't like it——'

'Am I being difficult?' It was hard to tell whether his expression showed injured innocence or amusement.

'Yes, you are! You started off wangling your way in by giving me the impression you were renting a bed, and I'd never see you, and now we're practically eating together all the time, and I won't have it, do you hear!'

'I hear all right—I can hardly avoid it. You make yourself very clear, Tania. I'm sure you're an excellent teacher——'

'Cut out the soft soap,' she hissed. 'And stop taking over my life for me!'

'Is that what you think? I was being helpful——'

'No, you're not. Helpful is what you're not. Bossy, yes. Taking over, yes—helpful—no. I lead my own life, you lead yours, and we'll meet as little as possible while you're unavoidably at *this* house—and I hope you get the water and electricity on at the Grange as soon as possible and that will suit me fine.' And she stared at him hard.

The telephone shrilled in the hall before he could answer, if indeed he had any answer to *that*. 'Excuse me,' said Tania, and went to answer it. It was Ted, and he was furious, that much emerged after only seconds. She had a brief, action-packed conversation with him, and slammed the telephone down. She glared at Bryden who sat eating his salad as if nothing was wrong.

'I hope you're satisfied,' she said, and plonked her dish in the sink.

'Why? What have I done?'

'Done? What do you ever do except cause chaos? It's all round the village that you've moved into the Grange. Ted's hopping mad and so's his father. They want to know what the hell's going on. I don't suppose you *knew* that his father was interested in buying the Grange, did you?'

He looked up. 'Did *you*?' he asked quietly.

'That's got nothing to do with it!' she flashed back.

'Oh yes, it has. Did you know?' he repeated.

Tania sat down. 'No, I didn't.' That had hurt her. Ted should have told her that at least, but he hadn't. She looked at Bryden, and some of the fire had gone. 'You knew?'

'I knew that some firm called County Construction wanted to buy. *And* I know what for. But I'll bet Ted didn't tell you *that*, did he?'

'What do you mean?'

'No, he didn't tell you, I can see. Well, I will. Mr Latham wanted to buy the Grange so that he could knock it down, and very possibly this lodge as well, and build an estate of holiday chalets——'

'Don't be absurd!' she gasped. 'I've never heard anything so——'

'I'm telling you the truth, Tania, whether you choose to believe it or not. This is prime land, only minutes from the sea, and East Yorkshire is very popular for holidays. Look at Scarborough—at Whitby——'

'But—a holiday village—here!' Her face was white.

'Not so absurd as you seem to think. I've gone into it. Your Mr Latham had it all thought out. There would be permanent homes here too. The estate is several acres. He could build dozens of the bungalows—and he'd already applied for, and got, the planning permission when he offered a price for the Grange and its gardens.'

'How long ago?' she asked dully. She felt numb with shock, betrayed by the man she thought loved her.

'About six months ago. He's been negotiating ever since, without success, I might add, which didn't please him. He's got just about everybody in his pocket—including your local council—but he hasn't got the owner of this house, who has now decided he's going to do up the Grange and live there, and there's nothing Jack Latham can do about that.'

Tania sat very quietly for a moment digesting the information. No wonder Jack Latham wanted her and Ted to marry! He knew—or thought he'd known—that the Lodge wouldn't be in existence for much longer. And the gardens—— She looked up at Bryden. 'The trees, those beautiful trees,' she said. 'You mean he'd just have chopped them down?'

'Every one, I wouldn't be surprised,' he said. 'That's life, though, Tania.'

'Oh God!' She looked down at her hands. 'I love it here—I couldn't imagine——' she stopped.

'I know. But it's not going to happen. The man who owns this house is Colonel Marchbank's grandson. He doesn't want a thing altered, except the house itself—and that only to improve. I've very detailed plans, I promise you, and none will spoil anything, only enhance.'

'I think he's coming round,' she said. 'He could be here any minute. I think you'd better go. I didn't tell him you were staying here—which is just as well now—but I'd rather deal with him alone.'

'Are you sure?' He looked at her. 'I'll go back to the Grange if that's what you really want, and keep out of the way until he's gone. But he's going to find out sooner or later that I'm staying—that's inevitable. Isn't it better to get it all over with now while he's still mad, than let it blow up later when all is calm?'

'I don't know,' She put her hands to her face. She was still shocked, and felt helpless, which was unusual for her. She heard a movement, then, the next moment, a hand on her shoulder, warm, reassuring.

'Then I'll stay,' said Bryden. 'I can hear a car now. Do you want to go into the lounge or stay here?'

'I don't know.' It seemed all she could say. He pulled her to her feet, very slowly, easily, and held her to him.

'We'll sort it out,' he said. 'Put a smile on your face.' He lifted her chin and she saw the dark strength of his features and was drawn towards him as helplessly as a moth to a flame. The next moment his mouth was on hers, hard and demanding and very sensual, and she was lost, drowning in a sea of the senses, unaware of time or anything else save the moment, and what was happening.

Then suddenly it was over, and she pulled guiltily away, eyes dark and wide and horror-filled. 'Oh!' she gasped.

Bryden touched her hair. He was not quite laughing but nearly. 'And very nice too,' he said softly. 'Just what I need before a fight.'

Then, as if on cue, the front doorbell was jabbed violently. Again and again it shrilled, angry, threateningly, filling the house with sound as Ben began to bark.

'You'd better go and answer it,' said Bryden.

CHAPTER THREE

Two men stood on the step—Ted, and his father. Jack Latham pushed in first, walked into the lounge and turned. Tania followed, Ted came last, closing the door behind him.

'Well, lass,' said Jack Latham, 'what do you know about the Grange, eh? Have you seen this fellow that's come from London?' His round, normally ruddy face was paler and taut with anger, though it seemed clear he was trying to control it in front of Tania. Probably, she thought, with a flash of sudden insight, so that he can find out more from me before he blows his top. She had closed the kitchen door when she went to open the front. Now she heard it open quietly, and her heart thudded. She could almost see Bryden walking quietly along the hall, waiting outside.

'Yes. He's going to work on it, make it habitable again.' She looked at Ted, who stood just inside the door, dismayed to see what was on his face. She felt sick.

'The man's mad! That place is a wreck—only fit for pulling down! I've said it all along.'

'Is that what you planned, Mr Latham? To pull it down?' she asked. All her fear had gone now.

'Is *that* what he told you? So you've been talking, eh?' He looked at his son, who had not said a word since coming in. 'Go and get him, Ted, I want a word with him. I want to know who the devil he thinks he is— showing George Medley his fancy bits of paper from a bloody solicitor's——'

'Did you intend to pull it down?' she repeated, cutting Jack Latham off in mid-sentence. Nobody ever did that to him. He looked at her as though she were an impudent child.

'Never mind that, Tania. You don't understand business——'

'I understand what I'm told. You'd pull this lodge down as well—but you never said a word to me about it.' She turned to Ted, who was looking distinctly uneasy by the door. 'You never told me, did you?'

'Because I told him not to, you silly girl. Never trust a woman with a secret. It'd have been all over town in five minutes. My plans are my own. Now, get him, Ted. I've not time to waste yapping here——'

'You don't need to get me. I'm already here.' The voice which came from the doorway effectively silenced Jack Latham, whose jaw dropped. Tania stood looking at the little scene like an observer, feeling a strange sense of detachment at it all, as though she wasn't really there. Ted just inside the room, turning slowly, his fair skin going paler at sight of the man standing there. Jack Latham for a moment bereft of speech—and Bryden, whose head nearly touched the top of the doorway, standing there quite calm, not quite smiling, looking at Ted's father.

'So we can talk, can't we?' He walked in, towering over both men, and looked calmly from one to the other, then at Tania. 'Do you want to stay?' he said.

'It concerns me, so yes,' she said, and sat down.

'Damn that!' exploded Jack Latham. 'This is man's talk—not for women. Ted, take her in t'kitchen.'

'You can boss everyone else, but you can't tell me what to do in my own house, Mr Latham,' Tania retorted. 'I'm staying.'

'You won't like it, I promise you that,' he snapped, glaring.

'Why won't she?' Bryden cut in. 'There's nothing you can do. I'm here to work at the Grange for as long as it takes me to renovate it. It doesn't belong to you and it never will, so there's really not a lot to say.'

'Isn't there, by God? You'll see if there's nothing I can do! You can't work alone, that's for sure, and by gum, I'll see you don't get any labour to help you! That's just for starters, lad. And then I'll go down and see your fancy solicitors next week and see what right you've got to be here, and who exactly does the house belong to, because I made a damned good offer for the place, more than it's worth, and I don't like being done out of anything, and I don't give up what I want.'

'Fine,' said Bryden. 'You do that. As for me not getting help, thanks for the warning. I'll have to cast my net a bit wider, that's all. I don't get beaten either—not by men like you.'

Jack Latham's eyes narrowed. It was a danger sign Tania recognised only too well. 'Men like me?' he said softly. 'And what precisely does that mean?'

'You should know already, but I'll spell it out. You're powerful in business because what you can't get by honest means you'll get by bribery—or buying people, to put it more bluntly——'

'I'll sue you for slander!'

'Try it. And I'll get proof. You can't buy me and you can't buy the solicitors who're dealing with the late Colonel's estate, so you're stymied, to put it frankly, Mr Latham.'

Jack Latham advanced on him, his fist raised. For a moment, a terrible moment, Tania thought he was going to strike the younger man, but he didn't. He looked very formidable close to, and that point must have occurred to Jack Latham, for he stopped only a foot or so away. 'By God, I'll break you! I'll get you out, one way or t'other. Nobody talks to me like that and gets away with it, d'you hear me?'

'I hear you perfectly. Have you said all you've come to say? If you have, I'll go. I've got work to do.'

'I've said it all for now—but I've not finished, not by a long chalk. You'll be hearing from me!'

'Good.' Bryden turned to walk out, glancing briefly at Tania as he did so. She stood up.

'I think you'd better go, Mr Latham. I don't like scenes like this.' She looked at Ted. 'Are you staying?'

He looked at his father before replying, then shook his head. 'No, I'll go home with my dad.'

At the front door she stood and watched them go down the path, then closed the door. She wanted to weep, but she wasn't going to. Something had changed now, and would never be the same again. She heard their car start up, and walked, dry-eyed and steady, towards the kitchen.

'I hope you're pleased with yourself,' she said to the waiting man.

'I'm sorry.'

'I'll bet you are! You look it! You were enjoying yourself in there, weren't you?' she lashed out.

'No, not particularly. That's the truth. I don't like that kind of scene any more than you do. Why should I? I want to be left alone to get on with what I came to do. But I don't like bully boys, and that man is a bully, even you must know that.' He stood straight and tall, not giving an inch, every word calm and reasoned—and true.

That was what hurt. He spoke the truth, and in his treatment of Jack Latham had showed up not only father but son as well. Ted had emerged in a very poor light. She sat down at the table and he said: 'Can I make you a drink?'

'Yes. Anything—tea or coffee.' She had no strength left. Certainly not to argue. 'Can he do that—go to the solicitor's?'

'There's nothing to stop him. I don't think he'll find much out, though. You know what solicitors are, they're very discreet. I'll telephone them in the morning and tell them what happened. May I phone from here? I'll pay for the call, of course.'

She nodded. 'Can he do anything?'

'He might have made an offer for the Grange and land, but that doesn't constitute a legal agreement, unless it was accepted.'

He spoke so calmly, as if nothing had happened. Perhaps, for him, it hadn't. Perhaps he was used to dealing with men like Jack Latham. Tania wasn't. She still felt inwardly sick at it all—and at Ted's apparent weakness after his anger over the telephone.

She took the cup of tea from him gratefully. 'He says he'll break you. Didn't it scare you? He meant it.'

'He's bluffing. Drink your tea. There's nothing he can do to hurt me.'

'You don't know him,' she said bitterly. 'He forced one man out of business in the village, a butcher who'd refused him something once—something so trivial I can't even remember—and in no time the man had scarcely any customers. He had to sell his shop and leave.'

'A pleasant fellow. No wonder you're not too sure

about him as a father-in-law. I'd think twice about that prospect.'

Tania didn't like talking to Bryden like this. It seemed terribly disloyal, yet there were so few people she had ever been able to talk to about him. Her best friend in the village, Beth, was completely loyal, but her husband worked for Mr Latham, which made the situation difficult. Tania sighed.

'What a mess it all is!' she said.

'It needn't be. Tell me honestly, which would you rather see? The Grange restored, or a holiday village with cars all over the place—and no trees?'

She shuddered. The question scarcely needed answering. And Ted had never said a word. He'd even made jokes about living at the Lodge when he must have known all along of his father's plans. She could remember how the Grange had been fifteen years ago when she had first come to live with her grandfather after her parents' death. It had been full of life and light, elegant and gracious, with well kept lawns. One night she had crept out of bed, dressed only in pyjamas and coat, because there was a party. She had watched from a good vantage point, hidden by shrubbery, seen the couples dancing on the floodlit lawn, heard the music drifting out, the clink of glasses and cutlery, the laughter ... It had been a vivid memory, never forgotten.

'Penny for them?'

She came back to the present. 'I was remembering the parties here at one time——' she told him about that one, and he listened attentively.

'Then I should imagine, when it's all done, those days will return.'

'How? Do you know the new owner?'

He smiled. 'Slightly. You don't think he'd employ a perfect stranger to do his house up, do you?'

'I don't suppose so. What's he like? Old—young— married?'

He frowned. 'Let me see. Under forty, I'd say, wealthy —bit of a playboy, I imagine——' he paused as she pulled a face. 'No? Doesn't appeal?'

'No, thanks. Not that he's likely to look at me any- way! Is he married?'

'He wasn't at the last count anyway. But you never know with the jet set, do you? They change wives like they change their socks.'

'I'm not too sure I want to meet him,' she said. 'You said before, something about him not wanting the Lodge. But how can you *know* that? He might want a gardener or someone living here.'

'Would that upset you terribly—to have to leave, I mean?'

Tania thought about it for a moment. 'I don't know.' She had suddenly realised she shouldn't trust him too much. She knew next to nothing about him, she didn't particularly like him. He had, after all, virtually black- mailed his way into her home. She looked up at him and gave a terribly casual shrug. 'I'll manage.'

'I'm sure you will. Now, if you'll excuse me, I'm going back to the house. I'll do my shopping in the morning. Anything I can get you?'

'No, thanks. I shop on the way home if I need to. Oh —how late will you be in tonight?'

'About ten? That all right? It'll be dark then.'

'So you won't need a key. I'll be up. I'll look one out for you tomorrow, though, so you can do your telephone call.'

'Thanks.' Bryden looked steadily at her. 'I did mean it when I said I was sorry. I know you didn't believe me, but I didn't like saying what I did any more than you.'

For a moment of time, an infinitesimal second, it was as though something passed between them, then was gone. When he had departed, Tania thought about it. It had been a flash almost of empathy, of fellow feeling, and they had both been aware of it, of that she was certain. It was odd, because she didn't like him, and yet for that moment she had been allied with him. She began to look out her papers in preparation for work.

She was watching the news on television when the ring came at the front door, and Ben started barking. Tania had been so engrossed in the play previous to the news that she had forgotten that Bryden would be returning, and she ran to the door to open it.

'Come——' she began. But it wasn't Bryden, it was Ted.

'Can I come in?' he asked, and it was instantly obvious that he had been drinking.

She opened the door wide. 'I didn't expect to see you again tonight,' she said.

'Who did you expect then? *Him*—that troublemaker?' He looked at her sadly. 'I've been thinking about him, and what I want to know is—what was he doing here before? I mean, he didn't just pop up out of the woodwork, did he?'

Tania steered him gently into the kitchen. 'I'll make you a cup of strong coffee,' she said. 'I think you could do with one.'

He shook her arm off. 'Don't patronise me, love. I'm not drunk, and I'm not stupid. What was he doing here?'

He had left the front door open, and Tania had let it be. She hoped, if Bryden arrived, as he could do any minute, he'd have the sense to stay out of the way until Ted had gone. She didn't think that now was the moment for her would-be fiancé to discover his enemy was actually a guest in her house.

'I need a coffee,' she answered. 'I've been working all evening. Don't be so touchy, there's nothing wrong with you having one as well, is there?'

Ted slumped on to a stool, dejection in every line of his body. 'Oh God, I feel terrible,' he groaned. 'Dad's been playing hell all evening, phoning round, putting the black on that man. He'll be bloody lucky if he can buy a box of matches in the village after tomorrow.'

Tania's heart gave a few erratic bumps. Ted's father was really pulling all the stops out. 'There are other places,' she said gently. 'I don't imagine that would put him off.'

'That's what I said, and he told me to shut up until my opinion was asked for.' He looked at her. 'I've a damned good mind to leave home.'

'Why don't you? You're nearly thirty.'

'Because I haven't got a bean, that's why, my darling. I work for Daddy, remember?'

'So? There are other jobs, you know.'

He took the brimming beaker of sweet coffee. 'Thanks. Easier said than done.'

'You said it first. If you don't break away soon, you never will.'

'I need you, Tania.' His voice broke with emotion. 'If you'd marry me, everything would be all right. He respects you——'

'It sounded like it tonight!'

'No, he does. He was so mad then he didn't know what he was saying—but he really respects you because you're not afraid of him.'

She heard a faint noise from the hall, and froze. Bryden. And if he came in. . . .

'Just a second, I'd better close the front door. It's getting dark.' She went quickly past the dejected man, closing the door behind her. Bryden was walking quietly up the stairs. She mouthed the words, 'Ted's here—he's drunk and upset—please keep quiet,' and he nodded and went on up. She closed the front door loudly and went back to the kitchen. How long had Bryden been listening in the hall? And how long could she keep his presence a secret from Ted? One night was easy, but there would be other times. . . .

'I think we'd better talk tomorrow—it's late and I'm tired. Do you want me to drive you home?'

'No. I want to stay here with you, Tania.'

That's all I need, she thought. Two men here. 'Better not,' she said gently. 'In the morning things will look different, you'll see. We'll talk things over tomorrow when you're——' she had been going to say 'sober,' but hastily said instead: 'feeling better. It's late now——'

'Don't you hear me? I *need* you—I *want* you—oh Tania, how I want you,' and he lurched to his feet and grabbed her. Oh God, she thought, I hope *he* doesn't rush in to rescue me, because I can cope with Ted but I'm not sure if I can cope with two of you, especially not now. She let him hold her, and he was raining kisses on her face, clutching her tightly—but all she felt was a pity, and an emptiness.

'Ted,' she protested, when she was able to speak, and breathe again, 'not like this—please, you're hurting me——' She kept her voice quiet, dreading it in case Bryden was eavesdropping, something she wouldn't for one minute put past him. But Ted was past listening.

'Come on, please, Tania,' he begged. 'Love me a little —there's nothing wrong in it. We'll be married soon— and you're driving me insane—how can you be so cruel?' His voice dropped and then, to her horror, he began to cry.

She had to get him in the lounge. With any luck, once there, in his condition, he'd fall asleep. Then she would have time to think what to do. She began to move, helping him along, whispering: 'Let's go and sit down and talk, love——'

It took several minutes, but at last they were sitting on the settee, and here Tania gently extricated herself from his fevered embrace, murmuring: 'I must go— won't be a minute, love, make yourself comfy. I'll be back——' She slid away from him and out of the door. There, outside, she waited, heart beating fast. She heard him mumble something, then silence. Still she waited until, after a minute, gentle snores issued from the lounge.

Her tense body relaxed. Now what? Then she looked up—and Bryden Kane was standing on the landing looking down at her. There was no expression of amusement, or anything else for that matter, on his face. He just looked at her, his features a studied blankness. She looked back from him and peeped into the lounge. Ted had fallen sideways on to a cushion sleeping like a baby. She ran up the stairs and motioned Bryden into his room. Then she shut the door. 'I suppose you heard?' she said accusingly, before he could speak.

'I could hardly avoid it,' he remarked dryly. 'What are

you going to do? Leave him there? He *is* asleep, isn't he?'

'Yes. I can't let him drive home in that condition—but you can be darned sure it'll be all over the village tomorrow if I let him stay. Daddy would see to that,' she added bitterly.

'Can you drive a car?'

She looked at him. 'Yes, just about—but he lives the other side of the village, about seven miles away. How would *I* get back home? I'm not asking his dad for a lift back. Not after that scene.'

'I can follow in my car. Leave him near his front door and I'll pick you up outside. Simple.'

'I don't know——' she said doubtfully.

'Oh, come on, Tania. You said yourself he's not fit to drive—and you certainly can't walk back alone at this time of night. Go and get him into his car and drive off slowly. Mine's up at the Grange. As soon as I hear you start up I'll dash off and get it. Stall outside the gate or something until you know I'm behind you. I'll flick my lights. Off you go.' He opened the door.

'But——' she began.

'*Go!*' he repeated. And that was that. There was something so assured about his manner that Tania ran downstairs before realising she was meekly obeying a man she didn't like or trust, and it seemed the natural thing to do. She hadn't time to think about the implications of that, for Ted was groggily half awake when she returned to the lounge, calling her name. He glared at her.

'Where you been?' he demanded.

'Looking after you,' she retorted. 'I'm going to drive you home. Come on, up you get——'

'Don't be silly—you can't drive——'

'Yes, I can,' she said firmly, praying she would remember which gear was which. She had had very little practice in a car.

'I'm staying—it's comfy here. Sit down.' He patted the settee beside him and leered sleepily at her.

'No!' She was fast losing her patience. 'You're *drunk*, do you hear me? And I'm fed up, and you're going home. Right now.' And she tried to pull him to his feet, without much success for he was a dead weight, not helping at all. 'Damn it,' she muttered, 'get *up*!'

Some glimmer of realisation that she was getting angry must have filtered through to him, for he looked at her almost soberly for a moment.

'You're cross,' he said in wonder.

'I damn well am,' she retorted. 'Now get up!'

'All right, all right. I can do without bossy women as well——' Muttering and grumbling, he went out, and she followed.

A few minutes later they were in his car. Tania switched on the ignition and they were off, very slowly towards the lodge gates, then out, a few hundred yards along the road where she managed to make a bad gear change and stall the car. Her by now silent passenger was already asleep, and when she saw a car emerge from the gates and briefly flick the headlights, she started off again with much more confidence. Everything was all right now. Bryden was following. It was as if seeing him had lifted a weight from her. She would think about the implications of that too, later.

The drive towards and through the village was uneventful. Few cars passed either way, and the pair of sidelights following steadily a few hundred yards behind were very reassuring. The tricky part would be when she arrived at Ted's house. She didn't want to go too near, yet she couldn't leave him too far away from the house because it was quite possible he would remain sleeping in his car all night if no one came out. A certain amount of finesse was called for.

As they neared his home, she flicked on the indicator to turn right and slowed down. As she drove in through the open gates, Bryden drove past them and for a horrible moment she feared he would just go on—but of course, he'd be turning further along. She was surprised at her own brief panic.

She coasted to a stop well within sight of the brilliantly lighted front door and put on the handbrake. Now, speed. As she got out, she tooted the horn twice, loudly, and ran down the drive. There, hidden in the shadow of the trees, she waited.

She saw the front door opening, a head looking out, and she fled.

Bryden was waiting outside, engine running, just past the gate. As she neared he opened her door and as she was about to get in, she was caught in the full beam of the headlights of an approaching car which was already slowing, indicator out. She recognised both car and driver in that split second before sliding into Bryden's. It was Jack Latham.

'Drive on, quickly,' she said. 'It's his father. Oh damn! He's probably been out looking for him and now he's seen me.'

'Does it worry you?' They were speeding along the road, and Bryden spared her a brief glance as he spoke.

'After all that's happened tonight? Not really. Things can't get much worse, can they?'

'You never can tell,' he answered cheerfully.

'Thanks a lot! You're a great comfort.'

'Just realistic.'

'Then you might as well know. When Ted came round he told me that his father's been making lots of phone calls tonight——'

'I know—I heard.'

'What? But he'd only just arrived——'

'I practically followed him in. I was in the hall for quite a while before you came out. I wanted to make sure you were all right. I could see he was—er—under the weather. That was quite interesting. The more I hear of Daddy the more pleased I am that he's not getting what he wants.'

'But don't you *see*? You'll have a job buying anything——'

'There are other towns. York's not a million miles away. You can't tell me he's got the citizens of that city in his pocket too.'

'No, of course not. But it's all so unpleasant.'

'That's my worry, not yours.'

'Thank the Lord it's Friday tomorrow,' sighed Tania. 'I don't fancy trying to teach lively eight-year-olds with all this going on.'

'You'll live. Think of the holidays.'

'I am doing.'

'Are you going away?' he asked.

'I don't know. Why?'

'I just wondered. If you're not—how do you fancy a holiday job?'

'Hah! Humping bricks? Knocking down walls? Super! I'm just built for that.'

'No, I'm quite serious. I'll explain when we get home —we're nearly there. Tell me where I turn, I might miss it in the dark.'

'About—see that large tree? A few dozen yards past that—slow down——' The drive in was accomplished without any problems, and Bryden switched off the engine. Ben started barking and Tania shouted him to be quiet while she searched in her cardigan pocket for her key.

In the kitchen she put the kettle on and turned to him. 'All right, tell me,' she said.

'It'll be secretarial work mainly. Invoicing, men's wages, phoning around for materials, etcetera.'

'That doesn't sound too difficult. And?'

'And—how are you on colour schemes?'

She stared at him blankly. 'What on earth do you mean?'

'I mean that the owner has given me *carte blanche* to paint and decorate as I decide, also to furnish throughout.'

'Good grief!' She sat down.

'And you, having lived here for years, can probably remember it as it was.'

'Oh, I can, very well. But times change—tastes change——'

'He's a traditionalist.'

'And a playboy? Come on! The two don't go together,' she scoffed.

Bryden looked at her very seriously. 'Think for a minute. Take the main dining room, for example. What colour were the walls?'

'Oh,' she frowned, 'a pale greeny blue—you know, that soft eggshell shade, and the ceilings were ornately plastered with the ribbon effect picked out in white——'

'And the carpets—and curtains?'

'Rich burgundy. There was a huge dining table and

chairs, a vast sideboard—all walnut, I think—and pictures on the walls——' The room was coming to life for her even as she spoke. She could see it so clearly it was almost as if she were there. 'And two chandeliers, very heavy in a deep silvery metal—I can draw them for you if you like.' She looked round for paper, and he handed her her notepad from the dresser.

'Now,' he said softly, 'do you see why I asked?'

Tania didn't answer. She was too busy sketching the chandeliers. And when she looked up, Bryden was smiling. 'Well,' he said, 'do you want the job or not?'

CHAPTER FOUR

THERE was really no decision to be made. Tania nodded. 'Yes,' she said. 'Oh yes, I do.'

'Good.' Bryden switched off the kettle and sat down beside her. 'Next week, once school's broken up, I want you to go through every room of the Grange and list everything you can remember about it and how it was. Everything, even inessential-seeming details. A lot of the original fittings are still there, of course, but not enough.' He looked at her, then he told her how much she would earn, and she gasped.

'But that's more than I get for teaching!'

'The owner is a very wealthy man, I told you. Money no object.'

'How lovely,' she smiled. 'I mean—not to have to worry about whether you can afford anything. Just go and buy it, and blow the expense.'

'Do you really think so?' He was looking at her in an odd way, not laughing, almost serious. So much so that she smiled.

'Yes, of course!'

'Why do you think he flits all over the world? I'll bet it's because, when you can have literally anything you want, you get bored.'

'Hmm, I'll try it for a while and let you know if I agree. You're not serious, are you? I mean, can you honestly say you'd rather be poor?'

'Not poor. But I wouldn't like too much money.'

'Oh, really! And have you got enough?' she retorted flippantly.

'Enough to manage on, yes. I don't think too much money brings happiness. Do you?'

Tania thought for a moment. Jack Latham had more money than anyone she had ever known, but she wouldn't call him happy, nor his family. She shook her head. 'You're probably right. It's not a problem I've ever had, to be honest, but thinking about Mr Latham—he's loaded, but he's not a contented man.' She smiled softly. 'My granddad, who brought me up, had just enough to manage on, and we were happy.' Her eyes filled with tears, and she turned away. 'I'd better make that coffee.' She despised the weakness that had brought the tears unwillingly to her eyes, and she busied herself at the coffee pot.

'This sketch is very good. Do you often draw?' Bryden might be hard and aggressive, but he could also be tactful, for which she was grateful.

'I like sketching, you know, nothing fancy.'

'That will be a big help. You could do drawings of the rooms as you remember them. Perhaps we could start this weekend? I doubt there'll be much else to do.'

'If you like. I'll have to warn the village children to keep away. The Grange has been a favourite haunt at weekends and holidays. They're convinced it's got a ghost.'

'I wouldn't be at all surprised.' He took the coffee from her. 'Thanks. I don't mind them playing in the grounds, but I won't want them in the house itself once work starts. There'll be too many tools and materials lying around. I know what kids are—particularly boys. I don't want holes drilled in walls where we don't need them.'

Tania laughed. 'I'll tell them you're a bit fierce—that'll keep them away. In any case it wouldn't do for me to be seen up there too often. *That* would be round the place like wildfire.'

'Point taken. Okay, say what you like. What will you tell Ted?'

She shrugged. 'I don't know. It's none of his business anyway. I don't belong to him.'

'Will you ever?'

She regarded him very levelly. 'No. Not even if I married him. Marriage is a partnership anyway, not a belonging.'

'You're very independent, aren't you?'

'Aren't you?'

'Yes.'

'Do you intend to get married—or are you already?' Two can play at your game, she decided. Let's see how you like personal questions.

'In answer to your second question, no, I'm not, and never have been, and to the first—I'll marry when I meet the right woman.'

'So you've not met her yet?' She raised her eyebrows. 'Tell me, what will she have to be like? I mean, you must have a mental picture of her—most men do, then spend years trying to match it. You'll want the submissive type, of course, blonde, big bosom, long legs and possibly not *too* intelligent——'

'Have you finished?' Bryden was trying not to laugh. 'What a ghastly picture you conjure up! Is that how you see my taste?'

'You're a very bossy man, or has no one told you? And yes, that *is* how I see your taste. Perhaps not the blonde hair, I don't know—but the rest, yes. And you wouldn't want anyone who'd argue with you.'

'That's a statement, not a question, right? So you assume that, do you? You're entirely wrong in all of it.'

Tania sipped her coffee. 'Oh, you mean you *like* arguing?'

'You're trying to put words into my mouth. I didn't say that. But I'd want someone with a personality to match mine——'

'Good grief! There aren't too many female Attila the Huns about!'

'You really are quite exasperating,' he observed. 'No wonder Ted's terrified of you——'

'He's not! How dare you say that!' She looked at him indignantly, eyes flashing.

'I dare because it's on about the same level as what you've been saying to me.'

'Oh well, if you're descending to personal insults just to get your own back I shan't stay and listen. I don't have to, you know. I shall just go to bed and let you chunter away to Ben. He'll listen to you. *He* likes you.'

'Even if his mistress doesn't?' he said softly.

She smiled. 'I'm working for you, aren't I? I shall keep my opinions to myself in future, and be very respectful ——'

'You'd die first. *You* respectful? Come off it, Ginger, that's exactly what you're not. You're as fiery as your hair——'

'I'm not! And leave my hair out of it, and stop calling me Ginger——'

'Whoa! You're working for me, remember? That bit of respectfulness didn't last too long——'

'Go to hell! I'm not working for you till Saturday, and not even then if you're not careful.' She stood up and glared down at him. 'So watch it, Buster.'

'Threats?' He stood up as well. 'Come on now, you want this job as much as I want you to do it. You love that Grange as much as you love this place——' he waved his arm—'and you always have—and don't try to deny it. I saw your face when you thought it was going to be pulled down. You were stunned—shattered. I saw that, remember, and I won't forget it. And you want the Grange restored to its former glory as much as the owner does, because I also saw your face when you were telling me about the party you'd peeped at when you were younger, and you were animated, reliving it as though it was actually happening.' He paused, and when he went on, his voice was softer. 'So let's not kid ourselves, Tania. You need this place as much as it needs you. Don't forget that.'

Tania sat down slowly. His words had had the oddest effect on her. All true, every one, and said in a way that prevented any effort of denial on her part.

Very quietly, she said: 'You're a cruel beast, but you're right. Oh, you're so very right.'

'I know.' Bryden sat down as well. 'I'll ignore the cruel beast bit. I'm hard, because I've had to be—and I get what I want. I always get what I want. Remember that, Tania.'

'Is it some kind of threat?' She was beginning to feel too tired to care.

'No, a statement of fact. I don't threaten women. I rarely threaten men, come to that—except when necessary. And with Jack Latham it might be necessary. You may have to make a decision soon that may not be easy. If—when—they find out what you're doing for me, your loyalties may be put to the test. This was why my seemingly personal questions before. I don't want letting down in the middle of a project. If you agree to work for me —as you have—and you start, I don't want you walking out in the middle because Ted puts pressure on you. Do you understand?'

It hadn't occurred to her that that was what could happen. Yet it was very logical and sensible. She clasped her hands. 'I won't let you down,' she said. She wasn't ready to tell anyone, least of all him, of the realisation that had come to her when Ted had been kissing her. She hadn't been sure if she loved him before. Now she knew, beyond a shadow of doubt, that she didn't, and never would. She could not marry him. And when the work was over at the Grange, and the new owner had moved in, she knew what she must do. She looked up at him, and the anguish was in her face, and he caught his breath as he saw her and said softly :

'Tania, what is it?'

It seemed right, now, at that moment, to tell him. She didn't question why it should be so. Very quietly she said : 'I won't be marrying Ted. I don't love him, I never have and never will. And—and when your job is done here, and the new owner moves in, I think I must leave here too.'

'My God! Why?'

'Because although I love it here, it's not my place and never has been.' The tears glistened, and she no longer cared to hide them. 'And life would be difficult for me in the village—he'd see to that——' She stopped.

'Where will you go?'

She shrugged. 'Does it matter? I'm independent—I've had to be. I'll manage. I like York. I might move there and teach, I don't know.' She blinked hard. 'Anyway, that's enough of my problems. They don't concern you.

I'm just very glad this place isn't going to be pulled down. I couldn't have borne that, and if Ted's father *had* bought it and done that, I'd have left him anyway.' She looked up at him. 'Perhaps you've done me a good turn, who knows?' She managed a weak smile. 'You've opened my eyes a bit sooner than they would have been, that's all.'

Bryden turned away. 'Oh God, what a mess!'

'Isn't it just? But then life is, some of the time. Cheer up. I think I'll have another cup of coffee. I'll probably stay awake half the night, but what the heck! I wouldn't be able to sleep anyway.'

'I'll make it,' he said, and they both moved at the same time and collided near the table. He laughed and caught hold of her. 'Sorry!'.

Tania trembled at the brief touch. She trembled because the memory of his kiss had suddenly returned to her, and she trembled because he was all man, vital and virile, and no one had ever had this effect on her before and it was quite devastating. She moved away, terrified lest he notice her shock, and stood leaning on the sink, supporting herself before she could find strength to make a drink. Bryden moved so that he was behind her, and she could feel the hard animal strength of him as he put his arms round her. 'Don't cry,' he whispered. 'Please don't cry.'

'I'm not,' she said, her voice muffled as he turned her to face him, and her head was against his chest, near his heart, so close she could hear his heartbeat, and she didn't want to escape, she would never want to escape again because she knew now, at last, why she didn't love Ted and never would.

'Oh God,' he groaned, and held her closely to him.

Tania's heart was beating like a sledgehammer. She knew she mustn't be there. It was all vaguely wrong. She didn't even like the man, but his effect on her was physical and immediate. When he kissed her again, she didn't struggle. She raised her face to his eagerly, her warm mouth responding in a way she had never imagined possible, her whole body aflame with a sweet longing she didn't fully understand, or want to, and his mouth hard, searching, demanding, was a threat to her reason, and his hands were the touch of fire, moving slowly, sensuously, awakening her body to new sensations. Helplessly, lost, she arched her body as his mouth touched a trail of ecstasy to her neck, her throat, her breast. . . .

'God, I want you——'

Sanity, cold sanity, returned, nearly too late, but not too late, and she found some kind of trembling strength and pushed him away.

'No,' she whispered. 'No——' Bryden's eyes, his face, were dark with excitement and passion, yet he stood back, and he too, was shaking. He rubbed his hand over his face, and whether he was angry or not, she couldn't tell. She didn't want to see. She didn't want to *know*. Sobbing incoherently, she ran out from the room and up the stairs.

Trembling and weak, she fell on her bed and buried her burning face in the pillows. What madness, what utter madness had taken her? She was under no illusions, not now, safely away from him. He would have made love to her, she knew, and she would not have stopped him, or even wanted to. She had wanted him to make love to her, had wanted it as she had never wanted anything in her life.

She heard no sounds from below. She knew instinctively that Bryden would not come up after her. Why or how she knew, she didn't question. It was a fact. Then quiet steps in the hall, his voice calling Ben, and the door opened, then closed. Tania went to her window to see Ben and Bryden vanishing towards the Grange. He was being tactful, giving her time to get to bed.

When, minutes later, she heard them returning, she was washed, undressed and sitting at the darkened window. He didn't look up, he came in and locked the door, and she heard them going towards the kitchen. She stood up, went to her door and wedged it closed with a chair. Then she got into bed. Her life had changed completely, and all within the last seven hours. Seven hours to change a life, she thought, that's all it takes.

It took ages for her to get to sleep, and when she did her dreams were vivid, dreams of the Grange years ago, with the Colonel, a kindly old man, prominent in them. He had given her, as a child, free rein to visit any time she wished. He lived alone, save for several staff, in the latter part of his life, but had often entertained relatives and friends, at which times she had, childlike, shyly stayed away. But she had sometimes watched the big cars going to the house, seen, from a distance, the fur-coated women, the elegant men who visited. Even then she had not been aware of envy, merely a vicarious enjoyment, a sharing in his happiness. And often, after the visits, when she called to see him after school, he would tell her who had been, and regale her with stories of parties, and often there would be a little gift that someone had left him, an ornament, a jar of exotic food—once, even caviar. She hadn't particularly liked that, but had been too polite to say so.

Physically frail, yet with a lively and youthful mind,

the Colonel played many a game of chess with her grandfather in the quiet winter evenings when no guests
stayed, and she had watched and learned, and been
allowed to play. There had always been a huge log fire
on those winter nights—her memories were very vivid
of the large drawing room, herself on a round leather
pouffe by the fire, a box of the Colonel's favourite mint
creams on a table near them, to which she was told to
help herself, and then, at nine-thirty or so, the housekeeper bringing in whisky for the two men and hot
drinking chocolate for Tania.

They had been happy days. To think of the Grange
being destroyed was even more unthinkable, in the light
of those memories, which all mingled with her dreams
and her waking times of that long night. And when morning came, she knew that when she began to work for
Bryden Kane her own recollections would provide the
essential key to the restoration of what had once been
a supremely beautiful house.

She drifted, she slept, she dreamed again, and more
recent memories surfaced, and were eminently disturbing—then a knock came at her door and she awoke from
a very confused image of herself and Bryden, at the
house. . . .

'Tania? It's nearly eight. Breakfast is ready. Are you
awake?' His voice was a shock, as if her dream had come
to life. For a moment she lay silent, and the tap on the
door came more urgently.

'Yes, I'm awake. I'll be down in a few minutes.' She
heard him going down and sat up, pulling the covers
from her. One more day of school—would she survive
it?—then two blessed days of freedom. With him.

She got quickly out of bed and put on her dressing

gown. A good wash would wake her up—and maybe give her the confidence to face him. She hoped so anyway. What had happened must be forgotten. Bryden was dangerous to her in ways he didn't know, but perhaps guessed. When she went up to the Grange, she would always take Ben with her in future—and she would avoid personal contact with Bryden as far as possible—difficult, but necessary.

Fifteen minutes later, dressed in her brightest lime green blouse and sensible grey skirt, she went downstairs to face him.

'Morning.' He spared her only the briefest of glances as she went into the kitchen. 'Toast's nearly ready, I've had mine. Tea or coffee?'

'Tea, please.' She sat down at the table. His manner was cool, efficient, almost as if a complete stranger were speaking—which, after all, he was.

'You said you'd leave me a key,' he said. 'I've a couple of telephone calls to make, but I'll place them through the operator and get the charges. Is that all right with you?'

'Of course. The spare key's in the vase on the lounge windowsill, if I forget.'

He handed her a plate with toast on, and she began to spread butter and marmalade on the pieces. She hadn't really looked at him. It was easier to look at Ben who sat patiently at her side waiting for his crust of toast.

'All right to take Ben out?' he asked.

'Yes. I leave the back door ajar for him during the day, and keep the gate to the run padlocked. No one can get in.'

'I noticed that yesterday.' He poured out two cups of tea and sat down. The conversation was stilted, polite, and quite as if they were two absolute strangers, met by chance, and with nothing to say. Perhaps they hadn't.

Tania looked at her watch. 'I must be going in a few minutes. I'll be back at four-thirty or thereabouts. Where will you be?'

'I don't know. It all depends how I go on on the phone. Either here or at the Grange, almost certainly.'

'Fine.' She nodded briskly. 'Er—if you do take Ben with you, lock the back door, won't you?'

'I will. Anything you want me to do? Vacuum—dust?' She thought he was being sarcastic, and looked at him for the first time that morning, but he wasn't. His expression was quite bland.

'Heavens, no, I'll do that when I get home. Were you serious?'

'Yes.' It was his turn to look surprised. 'I can turn my hand to most jobs. It would be no trouble.'

'No, that's all right, thanks anyway. I may take you up on that later.' She wanted to scream at him instead. 'Look at me! You tried to make love to me last night, don't you remember? Did it mean nothing?' The words were unsayable. She finished her tea and stood up, giving Ben his toast, and patting his head. 'Be a good dog while I'm away. I'll go out the back—my scooter's parked there. Goodbye.'

'Goodbye, Tania.'

She went out, closing the door behind her. Her hands were shaking as she tried to unlock the padlock on the gate, but she knew why. Minutes later, she was speeding down the road, thinking ahead to the day's lessons, putting Bryden Kane firmly to the back of her mind. The only trouble was that he refused to go.

*

She called in at the café Beth ran at lunchtime. The small place was crowded, as it was market day, and Beth was dashing back and forth with filled plates when she went in.

'Hello, Tania love. Go in the kitchen. Be with you in a minute.' She turned away. 'Right you are, sir, won't be a moment.' Tania smiled and went through the swing door into the large airy kitchen where Tony, Beth's elder son of nineteen, was busily cooking chips at the stove, and supervising a griddle of eggs.

'Hello, Tania,' he said. 'Seen Mum?'

'Yes. Need any help?'

'No, thanks, we're managing. Sit down—make yourself a cup of tea, kettle's on—there's a big pot should have some in, come to that. Want any egg and chips?'

She laughed. 'No, thanks, I'm not hungry.'

Beth dashed in at that moment. 'Phew! This is the busiest we've been all week. You would pick today to come! Two egg, chips and beans, Tony, and two sausage, tomatoes and chips.'

'Coming up!'

Tania poured herself a cup of tea and sat down again, knowing better than to speak while they were so busy. It would be impossible to talk anyway. Beth's place was a typical small village café, catering simply but well for the locals and, on market day, for farmers and people from outlying villages and hamlets. Beth ran it with two girls and, as today, her son, who was a student at Liverpool University and now on holiday.

The two waitresses came in with dirty plates and went out bearing pies and cream for the hungry farmers. When Beth next dashed in, Tania said: 'Look, I didn't realise you'd be so busy—I'll go——'

'No, I want to talk.' Beth glanced at Tony, who had his back to them, and put her finger to her lips. 'But it's difficult now, as you can see. Can you pop in after school?'

'Yes.' Tania lifted her eyebrows, and Beth nodded. That meant it was important. Her heart beat faster. She knew, with an inner certainty, what it would be about. 'Okay, I'll leave you to feed the masses. Thanks for the tea. 'Bye, Tony—don't work too hard.'

'I'll try not!' he laughed, then grinned at her.

As Tania and Beth went out, Beth whispered: 'I've been hearing things about the Grange——'

'I know. I was going to ask you—but I'll see you later.'

Tania had now to do her shopping in her lunch hour instead of after school, and accordingly went to the large supermarket near Beth's café and bought sufficient provisions for both Bryden and herself for the weekend.

The afternoon passed all too slowly, and at three-thirty Tania dismissed her class with a huge sigh of relief and went to the staff room to get her shopping. The headmaster popped his head round the door as she collected her things. 'Ah, Tania, thought I might see you. What's this about the Grange? Is it true it's been sold?'

'Well, in a way. Someone's come to work on it for a relative of Colonel Marchbank's.'

'Thank God for that! I'd have bought it myself if I'd won the pools, rather than let it be pulled down—oh!' It was as if he suddenly realised what he had said. Everyone knew she was going out with Jack Latham's son. Tania smiled, more to put him at his ease than anything. He was a nice man, unworldly and absent-minded, but with a good sound discipline that reflected through the school.

'It's all right,' she said. 'I'm glad too. I just didn't know that anyone else knew about those plans of Mr Latham's.'

'Er—well, I only found out by accident, I—er—know someone on the council, you see. He told me about the planning permission. It would have been a damned shame.'

'Well, it's not going to happen now. I didn't find out about that idea till last night. It was quite a shock.'

He looked at her thoughtfully. 'Yes, it would be. I'm old-fashioned myself—perhaps too much so. We need these old houses, and once they're gone, they can never be replaced. Just wanted to have the rumours confirmed. I'm very relieved. Well, off you go, then. Have a nice weekend.'

'Thanks, and you, Mr Martin.'

He held open the door for her. 'See you Monday—then only one more day, thank the Lord.'

Tania laughed, then paused. She had an idea. 'Mr Martin, do you know anyone who'd work at the Grange? Mr Kane—that's the man who's come to supervise the renovation—thinks it may be difficult to get help.'

She didn't need to explain why. He nodded. 'Yes, it will. I won't say too much—but we both know why. Leave it with me. I do have some contacts.'

'Shall I phone you over the weekend?'

'No, I'll call you when I know—or see you Monday.' He began to smile. 'Yes, I think I may be able to help. But not a word yet.'

'Not to anybody. Thanks, Mr Martin. 'Bye!'

Tania parked her Lambretta in the café yard and went in the back way. Beth was sitting having a cup of tea, and looked up. 'Hello. Come upstairs. The girls can look after the café ten minutes. Tony, you're in charge.'

'Yes, Mother, thank you, Mother.'

'And don't be cheeky.' Beth grinned at Tania. 'Nineteen! Would you believe it!' They laughed as they went up to the comfortable living quarters over the café. Beth, at thirty-eight, and fourteen years older than Tania, was a happy, plump woman with a warm personality. She knew everyone in Granchester, and was generally liked by all the villagers. She had taken Tania under her wing when she had first gone to live with her grandfather at the Lodge, and they now had an easy, comfortable friendship based on mutual regard and trust. Beth's husband Jim worked for County Construction as builder foreman, a quiet Yorkshireman but with his own strong opinions he was never afraid to voice.

'Sit down, love. You know what I want to talk to you about, don't you?'

'I think so. The Grange?'

'Ah, you do know? Oh, Tania, what's going on? Mr Latham phoned us last night, and he said some dreadful things. He said that a man, name of Kane, has arrived at the Grange and is going to work there, that he'd done him—Latham—out of the purchase, and that no one is to work for him, however much he offers, or he'll see they never get another job anywhere in building. It was a right carry-on, I can tell you. Jim nearly told him what to do with his job, he's not used to being spoken to like that, I can tell you——'

'He mustn't. Latham means it, Beth. We had a dreadful scene at the Lodge last night. He swore he'd get Bryden Kane out, and he meant it. He was frightening.'

Beth looked at her wide-eyed. 'Oh, Tania, that's awful! And you going to marry Ted. It makes life very difficult for you——'

'I'm not,' said Tania. 'Not going to marry Ted, I mean.'

She wasn't sure what reaction she expected, but the one she got took her completely by surprise.

Beth's face lit up. 'You're *not*? Oh, Tania, thank God, thank *God*!'

CHAPTER FIVE

TANIA rode home in a very bemused state of mind. The shocks and surprises were coming too thick and fast for her to take them all in. And Beth's reaction had been one of the biggest shocks to date. She had never said one word about Ted, had always welcomed him warmly on the rare visits they'd made to Beth, and generally appeared to like him. To discover, now, that she never had liked him, nor ever would, had shaken Tania beyond words. She and Beth were so close, yet she had never had an inkling of her feelings towards him. It had all come out, after those first startling words, and Tania had listened, growing more numb as she discovered why.

'But, Beth,' she had gasped, 'you never said a word before——'

'Because I thought you loved him. How could I? I detest his father—and I know what Ted's really like. He's shallow and selfish, and he's weak. He'd never have done for you. I can't tell you how relieved I am. Oh, I wish I'd been there last night when Mr—what's his name? Kane? gave him a talking to. No one's ever stood up to old Latham before. What's he like?'

'Mr Kane?' How did she begin to describe him? She looked at her friend, her dear loyal friend, who had never said a word because she didn't want to make Tania unhappy. 'You'd better meet him. I've a lot to tell you, Beth, but there's no time now. He's about thirty-five or so, tall, big, dark—a bit tough-looking—I thought he was a gipsy when I walked into the Grange and saw him. I was scared! He *is* tough too. I mean, he doesn't seem to be bothered about Jack Latham at all.'

'Tell him to watch out, though. Latham's a dangerous man.'

'And so is Bryden Kane,' Tania said quietly, suddenly aware of the truth of it, but unaware of Beth's comprehending eyes upon her. She saw only his face, his strong, dark face, and a shiver touched her spine.

'Yes, I'd certainly like to meet him,' said Beth equally quietly, and hid her smile, lest Tania see. 'I'll pop over on Saturday—just casually, you know.'

'Will you? All right.' And they had parted, after making the arrangements for a 'casual' visit on Saturday afternoon.

The house was empty when she went in, and Ben was in the kitchen waiting for her. Her eye was caught by a note under the telephone, and she picked it up. It was brief. 'Tania,' it said. 'I've made £14 worth of calls this morning. As I'd like to make more, I'll keep an account and pay you when you want. I'm up at the Grange. Bryden.' She put it down again. Fourteen pounds! Where had he called? Australia? Her usual quarterly bill was for not much more than that. She shrugged and went to make herself a cup of tea. Presumably Bryden's employer, the mysterious shadowy new owner of the Grange, would reimburse him. Money certainly seemed no object, and it was none of her business anyway.

She drank her tea while preparing tomatoes and cucumber to go in the salad. She was restless, and didn't know why. Normally, on reaching home on a Friday, she was glad to relax for half an hour, unwinding after a week's hard work, but today it was different. Too much had happened in too short a time. What was he doing at the house? Working?

It was no use. She put the cleaned lettuce in a colander, and called Ben. 'Come on, walkies,' she said. It was perfectly natural to go for a walk after school, and if Ben went near the Grange, well, she couldn't help *that*.

She locked up and set off, with Ben bounding ahead of her—and in the right direction. His car was at the front, and the door was open, a change from the previous day.

Tania walked up slowly, mounted the steps, and listened. There came a sound of hammering from a distant room, the noises echoing through the empty house. She called: 'Bryden?' and the hammering stopped.

'Upstairs in the gallery,' he shouted. 'Come on up.'

She called to Ben to follow, and walked up the uncarpeted stairs, her footsteps loud in the emptiness. Bryden was standing in the square gallery that ran round three sides of the house, hammer in hand, face black.

'I'm testing the wood,' he said. 'There's some that's rotten and needs coming out.'

'I got your note,' she told him, looking round. 'Did you find any workmen?'

'Not yet. My calls were further afield.' He wiped his sweating forehead, leaving a smear of white on it. 'There's a hell of a lot to do. When do you want to start work?'

'Oh, I thought tomorrow. You want me to begin today?'

'Just as you like.'

'I'll go and get my sketch pad. Do you want a mug of tea bringing back?'

'That would be splendid—if it's no trouble.'

'No. Stay here, Ben.' She turned and ran down again.

It was absurd, but she no longer felt restless. She felt alive, full of energy—and ready for work. Her fingers itched to be starting. She wanted to sing, but she didn't because Bryden would think she was mad, and she undoubtedly was.

When she returned, walking sedately because of the beaker of tea she carried, he was downstairs waiting for her. 'Come in the dining room,' he said. 'I'd like you to begin there, you have such vivid memories of it I want you to get them down on paper now. I found a chair so you can sit and work in comfort.'

He had indeed found a chair. It was a tall straight-backed dining chair of great age—and very dusty-looking. 'Sorry,' he said, as if he could read her mind, and produced a large rag and proceeded to wipe it all over. 'Right. Ready to go?'

Tania looked round her, memories returning. The walls were faded, the colour dimmed with the years of emptiness. 'Yes,' she said, 'I am.'

She sat down and opened her pad, then looked up at him standing there, just watching her. His presence made her uneasy. How could she draw with him there?

'Er—are you going back to your work? The hammering won't bother me, I assure you.'

He smiled slightly, as if he knew. 'You work better alone—why not say it?'

'All right. Yes, I do.'

'Fine. Shout if you need me,' and he went out.

I don't need you, she thought. Not in any way, and I hope I never do. She bent to her task, but suddenly it wasn't easy. Suddenly she didn't know where to start, or how. Ben sat by her feet, and Bryden was already upstairs, she had heard him go, and her mind and her sketch pad were equally blank.

She looked round her, seeing the room, seeing again how it had looked one evening she had called. There was going to be a dinner party that night, and Mrs Rennie, the housekeeper, had been supervising the laying of places, and had beckoned her in, explaining the cutlery settings, showing her how the napkins were laid, just so, allowing Tania, with her child's fingers, to fold one and set it exactly on its plate. A huge centrepiece of flowers lent the room a blaze of colour, and two candelabra, each with three red candles, stood at either end of the long gleaming white table.

Tania's eyes had been wide with delighted surprise. So many knives and forks! She had always thought one of each was enough, but not so. There had been a silver dish filled with sugared almonds on the sideboard, and Mrs Rennie had winked and given her a handful with the injunction, 'Not a word, mind,' and Tania had thanked her and gone to find her granddad.

It came back so clearly, so vividly, that her fingers flew over the paper now, as if some mental block had been removed. She drew that room as she had remembered it that night, flowers and candles, even the bowl of fruit and the one of sugared almonds.

So engrossed was she that she wasn't aware Bryden had come in until he spoke, quietly. 'Good grief, there's enough detail there! What's that?' he pointed, careful not to touch the paper with his dust-blackened fingers.

'A bowl of sugared almonds.' She laughed, and told him about them, and the dinner party, and her amazement at the variety of knives and forks.

He smiled. 'You've got total recall, do you realise?'

'No, I've not. Some things do stay in my mind more

vividly, though. The conservatory is another place I remember well. Most of the glass is broken now. Will you be doing that up for——' she paused. 'I don't know the new owner's name. What is it?'

'John Temple. And yes, he wants the conservatory filling with plants.'

'I've never heard of him,' she commented.

'Did you expect to have?'

'Well, you said he's a playboy jet-setter—they're usually in the gossip columns.'

Bryden laughed. 'Not all of them.'

'Will I meet him before he moves in?'

'I don't know. Do you want to?'

She shrugged. 'I'm working for him. Why not?'

'I'll let you know if he comes. I'm finishing now, the light's not good enough——'

She looked round. It was true, it looked as if it was going to rain. 'Never mind, I can do some more at home.' She stood up. 'Anyway, I'm hungry. Aren't you?'

'Yes.'

She was about to walk towards the door, hesitated, then turned back to the man who was looking out of the window. 'Bryden, is the Grange secure against intruders?'

He turned slowly. 'Do you mean what I think you mean?'

'Yes.'

'I've thought about it. At the moment, as you must know, it's virtually wide open. The locks are sound enough, but windows aren't secure. Let's put it bluntly because I don't like skirting round a subject. Do you think Latham would try a spot of vandalism—or even arson?'

'I wouldn't put it past him.'

'Nor would I. But he'd choose his time. He'd wait till we'd started work. On Monday this place will have certain security precautions organised.' He smiled, and Tania felt a cold shiver, seeing it. It wasn't a pleasant smile. Bryden Kane was ruthless, as ruthless as Jack Latham, in his own way.

She swallowed. 'Oh!'

'I made several calls today, as I told you. One concerned what we're talking about. Anyone trying to break in is in for quite a shock.' He walked slowly towards her. 'We'd better go. You've gone white. What is it, Tania?'

'You,' she whispered. 'You—frighten me.'

He smiled, his normal, slightly lopsided smile. Nothing unpleasant about that. 'Why? The bullies of this world have too much of their own way. Nobody threatens me and gets away with it. Jack Latham is a despicable kind of bully.'

'I know. I already know that—but——'

'But what?'

'You're as—ruthless as him—in a way.' The words were scarcely to be heard.

'Yes, very probably. But with one big difference.'

Tania looked up at him. Only a foot or so away, he towered above her, all-powerful, near, too near, yet she could not move, and didn't want to. She felt the strength of him surrounding her, encompassing her in a kind of wave, and this was where she wanted to be. Her heart beat rapidly with her nearness, and her head felt as light as if she might float away. No one had ever had this effect on her before.

'What is it?' she whispered, drowning in the sheer magnetism of him, wanting him to touch her, wanting to touch him, afraid, and yet not afraid.

'He seeks personal power. He already has it, and he wants more. He's corrupt. I seek no power, nor gain. I've seen what it can do to a man, and I want nothing of it. But what I guard, I guard well.'

'You say you don't seek power. Don't you know that you already have it?'

'Do I?' he smiled. 'What makes you say that?' He touched her arms with his hands, touched her so gently, yet her arms tingled at the featherlight caress.

'I've seen it—with them, last night, when you stood in the doorway. I shivered inside, I felt the power and strength you exuded——' He halted her by putting his fingers under her chin and tilting it up slightly so that her eyes were forced to meet his.

'I wasn't aware of it. Do I frighten you, Tania?'

'Yes. Sometimes.'

His wide mouth curved slightly, not exactly a smile, but the beginnings of one. 'You must tell me if so. I have no taste for frightening women.'

She must break the spell before it was too late. Didn't he know the effect he had on her? She stirred, moved restlessly, and he released her. 'We'd better go,' she said. 'Please.'

'Of course.' The spell was broken, she found the power in her limbs to move away from him, towards the door to find Ben, who had wandered off. He followed her out, then locked the door, and outside it was cooler, and the sun had disappeared, and she wondered what would happen when his work was finished and he had left the Grange for ever. There would be an emptiness in her life. Yet she had known him for a mere twenty-four hours. If he could do this in one day, what could he do in the weeks he would be there?

'Would you mind if I stayed in this evening? If you're in the lounge I'll work in the kitchen. I don't want to be in your way.'

'Work? What kind?' It was quite safe now. The subject of work was very safe ground.

'My plans for the major work to be done.'

'Ah. I thought *I* was employed for secretarial work?' They were walking towards the Lodge, through the beautiful trees, some hundreds of years old, and the huge branches heavy with leaves, provided a canopy of rich greens above them. Ben bounded ahead like a puppy, perfectly at peace with the world, no complications in his life.

'Yes, but not officially yet——'

'I've started sketching,' she retorted.

'Do you want to help?'

'There's nothing on television, and I've nothing to read, so I might as well.'

He laughed. 'Fair enough. I don't want to overwork you, that's all.'

'You won't. I mean, I'll tell you if you are.' It would be enough to be working with him—to *be* with him. She had scarcely thought of Ted all day.

Which was why it was such a shock to see his car parked outside the front of the Lodge, and him in it. Tania froze. 'Oh no!' she muttered. He had seen them, was getting out, looking at them both.

'Do you want me to discreetly vanish?' Bryden asked very quietly.

'No. There's no point in pretending you're not staying here. He must be guessing something by now. We might as well get it over with.

'Hello, Ted,' she went on, Bryden walking more slowly

so that she left him behind. She got out her key. 'You'd better come in.'

She opened the front door, and Ted followed her. 'Where's he going?' he asked.

'He's staying here.' Tania waited for the explosion as she led the way into the kitchen, but none came. Ted sat down at the table.

'What do you mean?' He looked at her, and he was more puzzled than angry—yet.

'What I said. He can't sleep at the Grange yet, because there's no water or electricity. So he asked me if I'd put him up here.' She heard Bryden close the front door, then him going into the lounge.

'You mean he's sleeping *here*?' Ted's handsome face was slightly pale, as if in shock.

'Yes. In the back bedroom.'

Ted's eyes were on her. 'Oh, my God,' he muttered. 'How *could* you?'

'I know it's rather unconventional——'

'Oh, it's that all right! *So* glad you appreciate the fact. Well, you can tell him to buzz off. I don't give a damn if the Grange is infested with rats, let him bloody well sleep *there*—he's not staying here.'

'But he is.' Tania looked at him, and she felt actually sorry for him.

'I don't want shopsoiled goods!'

She froze. 'What *do* you mean?' she said, controlling her temper with difficulty.

'You know fine well. You've never let me touch you —you've never let *me* stay here——'

'You've a home of your own.'

'You know damned well what I mean!' Ted stood up, shaking with fury.

'I'm not sleeping with him if that's what you mean,' she blazed back. 'And if you've just come for a fight, you can leave. I'm not in the mood for one—there was enough trouble here last night with your father——'

'And there'll be more, don't you worry. Wait till he hears about *this*!'

'Oh, so you're going to tell him, are you? Run to Daddy like a little boy——'

'Shut up, Tania!'

'I won't shut up in my own house!'

'But it's not *your* house, is it? Or didn't you know that?' He faced her, eyes lit with a kind of triumph that made her feel almost ill. 'And when the new owner arrives you'll be out so fast you won't know what hit you!'

'I suppose your father discovered that when he was making plans to buy and destroy the Grange,' she said, white-faced. 'And I suppose he thought it would make me marry you. Well, I've got news for you, sonny boy— I wouldn't marry you now if you were the last man on earth. Go and run and tell Daddy *that*. He'll be able to sell the marvellous house he's building for us—unless you want to go and live in it on your own!'

'You bitch! You *bitch*!' She thought he was going to strike her, and she backed slightly, physically frightened of him.

'Get out, Ted. I don't want to talk to you.' She turned away from him, unable to stand the look in his eyes. He whirled her round and shook her.

'I haven't finished with you——' he muttered.

'Let me go!'

'I could kill you! You've strung me along all these months, playing hard to get—little Miss Pure—oh God, you really had me fooled—and the first man who comes along, you let him——' Tania wrenched herself free, and backed, and he followed. 'Is that how you like them? Rough, like him?'

She hit him hard, and Ben, who had been watching huddled in a corner, growled and advanced on Ted, his fur raised, his eyes dangerous. 'Get out before Ben goes for you,' she snapped. 'You make me sick—you disgust me!'

Ted slapped her on her face—and Bryden walked in, took hold of him and knocked him down with one flat-handed blow to his chin. Then he hauled him to his feet as Tania grabbed Ben's collar and said, his voice low and menacing: 'You heard the lady. Get out. And if you ever touch her again, I'll kill you.' He shook Ted, then hauled him towards the hall. 'You're leaving now.'

She heard the front door slam, and they were both outside. Too shaken to follow, Tania sat down, still holding the agitated dog. 'It's all right,' she said. 'It's all right, Ben. He's gone.'

She could hear voices from outside. The deep tones of Bryden, Ted's voice raised. She couldn't hear the words, and she didn't want to. She just remained where she was, feeling, in spite of all that had happened, a desperate kind of pity for Ted, and the person he had become. She knew now that marriage with him would have been disastrous, which was why, instinctively, she had kept putting him off. And now it was all over.

She heard the door open, then Bryden walked in. 'He's gone. I'm sorry.'

'Sorry? For what?' She looked up.

'That it had to end this way.'

'Are you?' Her eyes were bright, too bright.

'Yes, truly. I sense that, underneath, he's not all bad. Not like his father. He's weak—but he should get away from him before it's too late.'

Tania didn't look at him. 'Have you any spirits in?' he asked. 'Whisky—brandy?'

'In the cupboard in the lounge, near the television.' She thought he wanted a drink, but when he returned with a bottle of whisky he poured her a small glass.

'Here, have that. It'll do you good.'

She sipped, too listless to disobey. She saw him looking round. 'We'd better eat. Let me wash my hands and I'll put the salad out. You need food.'

'I'm not hungry.'

'You were before. You'll be ill if you don't eat.'

'I couldn't,' she protested. 'Not now.'

'You can and you will.' Bryden began soaping his hands at the sink.

'Nothing affects you, does it?' she remarked. 'I'm sure you could sit down and enjoy a three-course meal if I put it in front of you.'

'Of course. And why not?' He turned.

'You're cold and hard.' She shivered, as if his coldness had touched her, and saw his expression change.

'You don't know me,' he said softly. 'You're prejudging.'

'I know enough. I've seen you in action.'

'I can't alter your opinion, and I won't try. If that's how you see me, so be it.' He shrugged.

'He knew what he was doing when he picked you for the job,' she observed.

'Who? Temple?'

'Yes. Did he know there'd be opposition?'

'Why should he? I didn't till I came here. Only that someone else wanted to buy. That happens all the time in business.'

'Why is he settling down here of all places?' she asked.

'Maybe he's weary of his playboy existence. You'll have to ask him when you meet him. I should imagine he'll arrive in style when he does come. He has a helicopter. One of my major jobs is organising the clearance and levelling of what used to be the bowling green at the back of the Grange.'

'Well, of course, what else?' she murmured. 'Doesn't everybody travel by helicopter these days?'

He looked hard at her. 'That annoys you?'

'No, not particularly. Why should it?'

'I detected a note of sarcasm in your voice.'

'I'm sorry, that was childish of me. I admire him in a way for what he's doing—keeping the Grange in character. I'm just not used to meeting the kind of people who hop in and out of helicopters as though they were taxis.' She looked at him and smiled. 'I've led a very quiet life, and it suits me.'

'And that's probably what he wants. As much as it's possible for someone with his money.'

'Doesn't it annoy you that you'll be doing all this work, seeing the place come to life again, for someone else?'

He smiled. 'It's a challenge. Any work is a challenge. I do the best I know how—that's my satisfaction. Don't you?'

'I teach to the utmost of my ability. Sometimes I wonder if it's worth it.'

'Do you? Don't you know it is? You must know.

Teaching must be one of the most rewarding jobs ever.'

'Hah! Don't tell me you've been a teacher as well?'

Bryden shook his head. 'No. I told you, I'm a jack of all trades.'

'I don't believe that. And if you are, it's only because it suited you. I imagine you've gone through life doing exactly what you wanted to do.'

He had finished preparing the salad and was buttering bread. 'Possibly,' he agreed.

'And after the Grange, what then?'

'Who knows?' He was busy finding the knives and forks, and he was smiling. He sat down opposite her. 'Eat up now. Then work.' Tania began to eat. 'The same applies to you,' he said. 'You'll be working just as hard as me. How do you feel about doing all that for someone else to walk into?' She hadn't thought about it from her own angle. He had the ability to make her see things in a new way. She thought for a moment or two.

'Yes,' she said, 'I see what you mean. It *is* a challenge. I suppose—I'll be only too pleased to know that the Grange is once again the beautiful old house that it was.'

'Good. Remember that. You'll never regret it, I promise you.' And there was something in his words, something that made her catch her breath, and a kind of awareness filled the room, and it was as if, just for an instant, she saw something rich and wonderful. Her heart beat faster. The moment had gone, but something lingered. She looked at him, and the awareness was in his eyes too, and he smiled. To ask, to shatter the feeling with words, was impossible. But something had changed in that instant of time. He makes me see things I don't fully understand, she thought. Just by the simple use of words. He has depths to him I don't even know, and I accused him of being cold and hard, but he's not. That's only a part of him, sometimes, and then, at others, he's so different, so very different. She kept on looking at him, because she knew she didn't want to look away, and she didn't care if he knew. Truly she had never known anyone like him.

'I'm sorry,' she said. 'You're not cold and hard. You may appear to be, at times—but there's a lot more to you than that. You were right, I was prejudging.'

'You don't need to apologise, Tania. You were upset—I understood that. I've had to be hard, because sometimes it's the only way to survive. But I'm not cold. I care about things I couldn't even begin to tell you, and they are an essential part of me. And I suspect that you're the same in a lot of ways.'

Tania wanted to cry. She didn't understand why, but he reached her, and his words had the power to disturb her, and she wasn't ready to know why—not yet.

'We're getting very deep,' she said with an attempt at lightness. 'All this at teatime too!'

'True. Then we'll change the subject. Work, I think. Can we work at this table afterwards? I've got plans to draw—and you've got notes to make.'

'Yes. Have you paper?'

'Plenty, upstairs in my luggage. I came prepared.'

'That's good. Have you contacted the Water Board and Electricity Board?'

'Both, this morning. They'll be here on Monday, but I suspect the Grange will need rewiring before anything else is done.'

'That could take a while,' she pointed out.

'I know. I've been on to a firm of electrical contractors in York. They'll be here too on Monday.'

'You've got it all organised!'

'Not yet. It soon will be.' He had finished eating, while she was scarcely half way through her salad. 'I'll make coffee. Eat up. No work till you've finished every bite.'

'Oh God, you sound like me when I'm on school dinners,' she groaned, and he laughed.

'Don't remind me of those. A plate of stodge, followed by prunes and tapioca—ugh!'

'It must be the same everywhere,' she said. 'I take sandwiches usually. I forgot today. They break up on Monday anyway.'

'And then it's all systems go.'

'Yes. I'm looking forward to it, I really am.'

'You'll do a perfect job, I'm quite sure of that. Your sketch of the dining room was superb. There's an auction in York next week of country house furniture. I'd like to go to it and see if we can pick up any pieces. I'd like you to come with me Tania, if you will. You'll spot anything straightaway.'

York? With him? Yesterday she would have laughed at the idea. Now, it was different. 'I'd like that,' she said.

'Then it's a date. Wednesday afternoon. We'll go in the morning for the preview, have some lunch, and back to the auction rooms.' He filled the kettle, and she watched him, watched his back. She wondered why she suddenly felt absurdly happy.

CHAPTER SIX

SHE staggered into bed at eleven after an evening of hard work. Bryden offered to take Ben out for his last walk of the day, to which Tania was only too happy to agree. He hadn't spared himself, and he hadn't spared her. He was a human dynamo when he got going, and Tania's hand ached with all the writing she had done. Her last coherent thought before falling asleep was—it'll be lovely in York on Wednesday, if I live that long.

She awoke to hear the birds chorussing their morning song outside in the trees, and the sun streamed in through the window after a night of rain. She felt gloriously alive and rested after a sound sleep, and stretched herself luxuriously before getting out of bed.

She would be going up to the Grange later when her own domestic tasks were done, she decided as she went to her door and opened it. Then she stopped as a very familiar whine came up the stairs. It looked as though part of her chores were already being done. The sound she could hear was of the vacuum cleaner, and someone —she needed only one guess as to whom—was plying it very busily over her carpets. She leaned over the banister rail to see Bryden vacuuming the hall.

'Hey!' she shouted. He looked up, then switched the motor off. It died down and coughed into silence.

'Yes?'

'I'm not paying you for that, you know,' she said.

He laughed. 'I know. I'm enjoying it, don't spoil my

fun. I can't find your polish and dusters, though. Where are they?'

'I'll be down in a few minutes.' She turned back and he switched on again. What an incredible man, she thought. He hadn't offered, he'd just got on with a chore she found boring but necessary. She was downstairs within ten minutes to see the kettle boiling away, the toaster on, and the kitchen gleaming smart and tidy. Bryden followed her in from the lounge.

'Good heavens, how long have you been up?' she asked, looking round at the immaculate working surfaces.

'About an hour. I've even taken Ben out. I saved the vacuuming till last so as not to wake you.'

'I could employ you on a full-time basis if this is the way you go on. All I can say is thank you very much.'

'Look, while I'm here I'll do my share, okay? And housework is such a novelty for me, I'll do it any time you ask. I made you work hard last night—don't think I don't realise. Now, sit down, breakfast is served.'

'Right. You're the boss.' Tania sat down. She had never realised how nice it was to be waited on. It had never happened before. She told him so, and he grinned at her.

'I do have an ulterior motive, you know.'

'I knew there was a catch in it somewhere. Go on— what is it?'

'Nothing very sinister. You're more valuable to me with your work at the Grange. I want you to keep your energy for that.'

'That's fair enough. Is that it?'

'Yes.'

'I don't see any ulterior motive there. And I am getting paid for that. Er—I was going to clean the windows this morning——'

'You're a slave driver, aren't you? All right. Eat up—

just tell me where everything is.'

'Bucket under the sink, chamois leather on top,' she answered promptly.

'I hope you'll enjoy watching me work while you sit there and eat your toast and drink your tea like a lady.'

'Oh, I will,' she assured him.

'I thought you might.'

Bryden began whistling as he started to clean the kitchen windows, and he worked very quickly and efficiently. Then outside. Tania ate while she watched him and when he vanished she began clearing away. She hadn't been going to clean the outside windows, although they needed doing, but there was no way she was going to stop Bryden from doing them.

Then a very odd thing happened. It was some twenty minutes later, and he had worked his way round all the outside downstairs windows and had come in to fetch clean water to do the rest of the inside windows, and Tania, feeling a slight twinge of guilt at letting him thus work, made him a cup of coffee and took it in to where he worked in the lounge. She moved the photograph of her and Ted taken at a tennis match from the table by the window and said accusingly:

'Now I know how you knew what Ted looked like— you'd peered through the windows!'

Bryden began to laugh. 'Did you really think I'd got second sight? Yes, I admit it, I——' he stopped. Outside, passing the Lodge at a crawl, was a white Mercedes sports car. A moment later it was gone towards the Grange, but Tania had seen Bryden's face in that split second when he had first become aware of the car—and she had seen the utter shock on his features before he could conceal it.

'Who was it?' she whispered, shaken. For one moment

this was not the man who was always in complete control of every situation. He had looked almost frightened.

He looked at her, his expression once again normal. 'I don't know. But I'm going to see. I'll do this later——' He went out even as he was speaking, and Tania was left with the feeling that he had completely forgotten all about windows.

She picked up the coffee he had also left, and drank it, and while she did so she wondered who had been in the car—and why. Why should anyone come here, unless it was to see Bryden? And why should there have been that shock on his face? She hadn't imagined it; it had been very real. Yet he was not a man easily shocked —and she would have said that nothing frightened him. She was uneasy, and, to make it worse, didn't know why. She couldn't remain there, not knowing. There was only one thing to do, and that was to go up to the Grange. She would take Ben. A dog was always a good excuse for a walk, and if he happened to go into the Grange, so much the better. She was going to make sure that he 'happened' to go there. Thus decided, she felt easier in her mind.

She whistled Ben. 'Come on, walkies!' she called, and he raced along the hall, skidding along the carpet and nearly crashing into the door in his enthusiasm. Tania had no idea what she would say to Bryden. But she was worried and that was more important than anything.

Ben ran on ahead, following Bryden's trail, and she walked quickly and saw the car parked at the front of the house. The door was open, but of Bryden and his visitor there was no sign. Ben saved her the trouble of any subterfuge by running into the house. Heart beating fast, she followed him in—and stopped.

Bryden was coming out of the dining room, and with

him was a most gorgeous-looking dark-haired girl, and she was laughing. Tania froze in that moment before they saw her, and the girl, her hand on his arm, was saying: '—you're an idiot——' then was stopped. Bryden had seen her, and had silenced the woman by speaking over her, cutting her off:

'Tania! We were just coming back to the Lodge.' He didn't look like a man who was frightened or shocked any more. He looked as though he had been enjoying a good laugh. The girl turned towards Tania, and she was older than she had appeared to be in that first split second of sight. She was nearer thirty than twenty, and she was extremely elegant in a swirly gipsy print dress and high-heeled spiky sandals. She made Tania, clad in her jeans and T-shirt, feel instantly gauche and juvenile.

'Hello,' said the woman, and walked towards Tania with hand outstretched. 'You're Tania and I'm Margo Temple.' She smiled at Tania, and while her face was friendly, Tania could feel a quick assessment being made.

Bryden spoke again: 'This is the owner's sister, Tania. Come to see if the slaves are working——'

'You have such an elegant turn of phrase, darling,' Margo said, and laughed. 'Bryden thought you might be kind enough to make us a coffee or something. I must admit I'm dying of thirst.'

'Of course. If you're showing Miss Temple round, Bryden, I'll go and put the kettle on——' Ben was busily sniffing at Margo's sandals, and she bent and stroked him.

'What a lovely dog! Do call me Margo—I hate formality. We've seen round, haven't we, Bryden? We'll walk back together.'

Tania swallowed. She needed time to recover—alone. Needed time to get her suddenly shattered confidence back. This woman—the *owner's* sister—clearly knew Bryden well. Much better than her brother? 'Of course,' she said. It was difficult to hide the sudden painful pang that had assailed her. Like a knife stabbing her heart, the feeling was quite new to her, but instantly recognisable.

'I must admit,' said Bryden, as he held the door wide open for them to go out, 'that I got a shock when I saw your car. I mean—so *soon*. Don't tell me you dashed up from London especially to see me?'

'Sorry to disillusion you, precious, but I was spending a weekend in York with the Melvilles—friends of the family, and I thought, I'll just go and see how old Bryden's getting on at the Grange.' They were walking down the steps now, and Margo spoke to Tania. 'I've visited here often in years gone by. Bryden tells me you're helping him to restore it to its original condition. I think that's a *super* idea. It always was a beautiful place.'

'Yes, I know. I'm doing sketches from memory,' Tania answered. To be asked questions about the Grange was easier than having to cope with the seething emotions inside her. She was sick and afraid. Had she really imagined that a man like Bryden would have no women friends? She hadn't given it a thought. He was here, that was enough. He had suddenly come into her life, and now filled it in a way no one ever had. And now—this.

'Any I can see?' asked Margo.

'Give her a chance, Margo,' Bryden answered. 'She only started last night. Don't tell me you're a slavedriver like your brother?'

'You should know that better than me, dear,' murmured Margo, and winked at Tania as though they were old friends. 'Don't let *this* one overwork you.'

'I won't. I did one sketch of the dining room yesterday. You can see that if you like.' She found it difficult to talk normally. Her words came out stilted. Margo was so damned *elegant*, tripping along in those flimsy sandals, her dress swirling round her in filmy waves, her long dark hair glossy and bouncy.

As they went in the front door of the Lodge, and Tania waited to close the door, she saw the smudge of glossy lipstick on Bryden's cheek and felt her mouth tighten. She wanted to *hit* him.

'Oh, what a lovely house!' Margo walked straight through into the kitchen, looking round her appreciatively. 'I was always curious to see round it when I used to visit.'

'Do sit down. I think the water's still hot in the kettle, it won't take a minute.'

Ben flopped down at Margo's side, and Bryden pulled up a stool at the table to be near Margo, while Tania busied herself with the coffee, praying she wouldn't drop a cup. She felt incredibly clumsy.

She heard the rustle of papers, then Bryden: 'Here it is. Take a look at that.'

'Good grief!' Tania looked round at Margo's tone, to see her studying her sketch of the dining room. 'You've certainly got the touch, Tania—and a darned good memory. That sideboard is exactly as I recall it.' She perused the sketch, her face serious and intent, then tapped it with a slender glossy-nailed finger. 'Bryden tells me you teach. Do you teach art?'

'That among other things. It's a small village school.' Tania poured out the coffee and put it on the table.

'I always loved art—but I'm nowhere near as good as you.' Margo took her cup and sipped. Everything she did was graceful. I hate her, thought Tania. But in a funny way, she didn't. Either Margo was making a deliberate effort to be pleasant, or she was naturally charming. Either way it made Tania uneasy.

'How long can you stay, Margo?' Bryden asked.

'Must go soon, darling. The Melvilles are taking me out to lunch with some friends. As I say, I just popped down to see what was happening—if anything—because, you know me, I'm incurably nosey.' She laughed, showing —of course—perfect teeth that only accentuated an equally perfect tan. A golden chain bracelet jingled on her wrist, and Tania watched it in fascination. Somehow it seemed to sum the woman up. Sheer wealth and elegance and a glossy confidence that didn't come from women's weekly magazines, but from years of breeding. She stood up straighter. Damn my jeans and T-shirt, Tania thought. My figure's as good as yours. The wrapping may not be so expensive, but so what, I'm me. And she managed her first genuine smile since seeing Margo. It was an effort, but she made it. Margo must think a lot of Bryden to drive the thirty odd miles from York to see him, although in that slinky car she'd probably have done it in minutes, but he wasn't fawning over her. He didn't look like a man who loved her deeply. But then Margo might be one of several. And yet—a shocking thought came into Tania's mind, hastily dismissed as Bryden asked:

'Will you be coming again?'

'I'm due back in London on Tuesday. I doubt it, my sweet. I'll phone you—or you can phone me some time, let me know how you're getting on. And I'll report to my dear brother, of course.' She gave a sleek, catlike smile to Bryden, who grinned.

'You do that. Tell him I'm earning my money the hard way.'

'He'll be delighted to hear it.' She smiled at Tania. 'My brother's a lovely man, but so cautious my dear, you can't imagine!'

Bryden laughed. 'Tell him I'm sparing no expense on his behalf, then, to spend his money.'

'I will.' Margo finished her coffee. 'That was lovely. I must go now. Bryden, walk me back to my car, will you?'

'Surely.' He stood up. 'I'll be back to finish those windows, Tania, in a few minutes.'

Margo held out her hand. 'I've enjoyed meeting you, Tania. I hope we'll meet again some time.' They shook hands.

'It's been very nice meeting you,' said Tania, not completely truthfully, but you couldn't always say what was in your mind.

She saw them to the door, closed it, then did something she knew she should feel ashamed of, but couldn't have stopped even if she'd wanted. She flew upstairs and peered out of her front bedroom window to watch them walk up the path to the Grange. Safely hidden behind the net curtains, she watched them—and wished she hadn't, but it was too late.

They were both laughing, and Margo had her arm tucked in Bryden's. Tania could almost hear the laughter, and she hated him, and Margo—and most of all, herself. There was a shared intimacy in that laughter, and it was for them, just them; it excluded her. She clenched her fists and watched until they disappeared from view, hidden by the curve of the drive and the trees. Then she leaned against the cold windowpane, and felt the dryness in her throat and a burning in her eyes.

What were they laughing about? There could only be one answer: Tania. Perhaps Margo had sensed the truth of what Tania herself had only just realised. Perhaps it showed more than she knew. 'Oh God,' she whispered, and put her knuckles to her mouth. 'Oh *God*, she knows —and she thinks it's terribly funny——'

She was still there, at the window when, some fifteen minutes later, the white Mercedes slowed down outside the Lodge and the passenger door opened and Bryden got out. She saw him lean in again, heard the faint murmur of his voice, then he slammed the door, stood back, waved, and watched Margo drive away. And the shocking thought returned to Tania, now not so easily dismissed. If Bryden was a fortune-hunter, he was doing extremely well. Margo would undoubtedly be as wealthy as her brother—and he clearly knew her well, and she must like him to travel from York to see him when he didn't expect her. And Bryden was working for her brother, and would be for a while. He's a clever man, she thought. Very clever, and he plays it cool.

She heard his voice as he came in, calling her, but she didn't answer. She didn't want to answer him, or speak to him at all, or even to work for him now. She wanted to run and hide somewhere.

'Tania?' he repeated it, and he was in the hall again, after going in the kitchen. She had to answer some time or he would come up and find her.

'I'll be down in a minute,' she called. She kicked her chest of drawers. It hurt her foot, and it didn't make her feel better, but it was better than kicking him, because he would wonder why—and then he might guess.

She sat down at her dressing table and brushed her rich

auburn tresses until her scalp ached and her hair shone. Then, defiantly, she put on some glossy lipstick, and pinched her pale cheeks. Her clear green eyes, dark-lashed, gazed back at her, but she saw nothing of her own beauty, only the tanned face of Margo Temple, smiling at her, superior—assured. She stood up abruptly, and the dressing table stool fell with a thud.

'Tania? Are you all right?'

'Go to hell,' she muttered, went to the door and opened it. Taking a deep breath, she went down the stairs. Bryden paused in his task of cleaning the lounge window and looked at her.

'I heard a thud.'

'I know. I knocked something over.' She glared at him icily from the lounge doorway. 'I'm going to make myself another cup of coffee.'

'Good. All right if I do your bedroom windows?'

'Yes.' She began to walk away.

'Then I'll have another coffee too.' His voice followed her, and she put out her tongue as she stalked into the kitchen.

She heard him whistling cheerfully from upstairs as she drank her coffee. She looked at the cup she had poured out for him and thought, I hope it's cold, and I wish I'd got some arsenic to add to that——

He came in, stopped whistling and looked at her, then said, 'That mine?'

'Yes.' She glared at Ben, who had done nothing, and put down her empty cup. 'Is the door of the Grange open?'

'Yes. Hold on, I'll walk with you.' He sat down and looked at her. 'Tania?'

She turned slowly. 'Yes?'

'What is it?'

She raised her eyebrows. 'What is what?'

'The air in here is dripping icicles.'

She stood up and carried her cup to the sink. 'Really? It feels quite warm to me. Where's my sketch pad?'

'Behind you.' He stood up too. If you laugh, she thought, I'm going to hit you, and this time you won't stop me.

'Excuse me.' She had to pass him to get to her sketch pad and pencil, and he caught her arm, and said:

'All right, little ice box, what gives?'

Tania shook her arm free and her eyes raked his face. 'Nothing. You'd better wipe that lipstick off, the shade doesn't suit you.' And she walked away and out. 'Come on, Ben,' she called as she opened the front door.

She walked up the drive, and whether he was following or not she didn't care. He wasn't. She reached the Grange and went in, straight into the dining room to carry out the chair which she took into the drawing room, her second favourite. She sat by the window, made herself comfortable, looked at the window seat and decided to sit on that instead. Her back was to the window, the window seat was wide and quite as comfortable as a chair, and it gave her a long view of the room, which wasn't quite the angle she wanted but it didn't matter.

She pondered a moment where to start, then something made her look round and out of the window, and Bryden was standing outside, just watching her. She looked away quickly. He wasn't laughing; he wasn't even smiling, he had just been standing there—looking. She was sorry she had turned round. Her heart was thudding, and the sketch pad on her knee blurred and trembled.

'There you are. Is that window-seat okay?'

'Fine.' She didn't look up. She made the first few tentative strokes on the paper as if engrossed in what she was doing, and the next moment heard him walk away. She let out her breath in a long silent sigh. The atmosphere tingled with tension, and it seemed that it filled the entire house, not just that one room.

Came the sound of distant whistling, bangs and thuds and the occasional crack of wood, but Tania tried to shut her ears to it and began her own work. Ben wandered off after a while, but she was scarcely aware of him going.

Then, when her hand ached, she looked at her watch. It was nearly one o'clock. She was stunned. She had scarcely been aware of time passing at all. The drawing was coming along nicely, nearly done. Then when she returned to the Lodge she would enter every detail of colour, type of furniture in full description on another sheet. And soon, after lunch, Beth would arrive. Before, she had wanted Beth to see Bryden. Now, something had changed. And Margo had changed it.

She sat back to rest her tired eyes, and closed them, and it seemed to her that she heard again the echo of Margo and Bryden's laughter, and that the laughter had become mocking, taunting. . . .

'Tania, are you still——' he stopped in the doorway, and she opened her eyes and focussed them on him. 'Oh, you're there. I thought you'd gone when Ben came up. How's everything going?'

'Very well. I've nearly done. Then I'll go and write all the details down.'

'Good. I'll go now. I wondered—would you like me to go and get something for lunch from the village?'

'They'll be closed by the time you get there.' Tania looked again at her watch for confirmation.

'Is there a fish and chip shop?'

'Yes.'

'Do you fancy some? I do. I've not had any for ages.'

She shrugged. 'Then go and get some. I'm not bothered.' She bent again to shade in a corner of the sketch.

'What does that mean? You don't mind what I get for you—or you don't want any?'

'Do what you like—I don't *care*,' she said crossly. 'I'm not particularly hungry. Is *that* clear enough?'

'Perfectly.' Bryden walked slowly across the room and sat beside her. Tania, very ostentatiously, moved away. He was smiling, she could see that even though she was avoiding looking at him. And she could feel the instant tension flooding the room in waves that were intangible but *there*.

'Tell me,' he said in conversational tones, 'because I'm interested in knowing, what precisely have I done to cause this icy barrier that I see erected before me? And don't bother to tell me it's my imagination, because one thing I am not is stupid. Nor am I so insensitive to atmosphere not to notice that your manner has been decidedly frozen for the past few hours—ever since, in fact, Margo's visit.'

She stared at him. 'I hope you enjoyed your little joke,' she snapped, voice taut with anger. 'I mean, I'm not stupid either. I do know when I'm being laughed at, and oh boy, were you laughing when you left my house!'

He nodded. 'I see. So you assumed, did you, that we were laughing at you? And if I said that we weren't, I don't suppose you'd believe me?'

'No, I wouldn't,' she retorted.

'Then I won't bother to say it,' he answered, and there

was a harder edge to his voice now than there had been a moment previously. 'But I will tell you this. I've known Margo for a long time. We have a lot to talk about when we meet—as we did this morning. And I assure you we've got better things to laugh about than you.' He stood up. 'In fact I don't get any pleasure from laughing at people—you included, although by God, your behaviour is childish enough sometimes to warrant it.' He put his hand under her chin and tilted it up. 'Look at you now—eyes flashing fire, red hair practically sparking in sympathy—and all because you've gone leaping in with both feet, jumping to the wrong conclusions.'

Tania pushed his hand away and stood up, putting pad and pencil down. She didn't like being at such a disadvantage. 'All right, you've said your piece,' she shot back. 'Good for you! But don't think I don't know when I'm being weighed up, because I do. And Margo was——'

'She thought you were extremely talented. She said so——'

'Oh, that's nice! You were having a little chat about me, were you—in between laughing about whatever you were laughing about—and I suppose she'll go and give a report to her brother. Well, bully for you—and bully for *her*!' She took a deep breath and in that moment's silence he began to laugh. 'Oh!' she shouted, 'you——' Arms flailing, she lashed out at him, and managed to connect briefly before he grabbed hold of her. Then suddenly he was not laughing any more. He was dark and serious—and he was angry. A muscle moved in his jaw and he looked down at her, hard-eyed, unsmiling.

'You are one on your own,' he said, oh, so softly. So very softly and all the more serious for that. 'You really are.'

'Let me go,' she said, equally quietly, because she was frightened, and because she couldn't move because his hands were like steel bands on her wrists and he wasn't going to release her until he chose to. She wondered if he was going to kiss her, and she didn't want him to—or did she? Not after him kissing and being kissed by Margo.

'When I'm ready. You really are quite a little wildcat at times, you know. If we're going to work together— and we are, let's make no mistake about *that*—we'll have to learn to get along. And we won't if you keep having your tempers for no reason——'

'It wasn't for no reason,' she shot back. 'And are you going to let me go or not?'

'I've not decided yet.' He pulled her fractionally closer to him. 'I have the advantage of physical strength over you——'

'And you're a brute as well,' she retorted. 'Big deal! So you've discovered you're stronger. All right. I'll stay here until *you* decide to let me go. Why don't you go the whole hog and put me over your knee and spank me? That's the traditional way you male chauvinist pigs assert your——'

'Don't tempt me,' he said. 'You'd be asking for it if I did——'

'Oh, stop talking rubbish!' she snapped. 'You're just——'

He completed the move he had begun moments before, by pulling her those last few inches towards him. Then in one instant he released her from his grip and instead put his arms around her very tightly, bent her head back, and kissed her firmly on her mouth. For a few moments it was an insult, that kiss—it was a punishment for her temper. Then, suddenly, it wasn't. So subtly did it

change that she wasn't aware of it until it was too late
to matter. The heady physical sensation was all that
mattered then, the knowledge of his arms around her, so
strong, so devastatingly strong, and aware; his face, that
face she knew as well as her own, ever since he had
come into her life, touching hers—his lips—the lips of a
man who knew what he was about in the kissing game,
and was well aware of it. Sensual, experienced, he knew
all right the effect he was having on her. And one small
core of sanity was retained, because Tania remembered
what had happened before and was frightened. He knew
too much. The only thing he didn't know was that she
had foolishly fallen in love with him—but if she wasn't
careful, he'd soon know that.

She struggled, but vainly. She struggled because she
hated him for her own treacherous weakness, and because if she didn't she would be lost—but it had the
opposite effect from what she intended. She sensed his
growing awareness and excitement, heard his quickened
breathing, felt his rapid heartbeats, and knew, despite
everything now, a growing sense of her own excitement,
a sense of power mingling with it—a truly heady mixture
of such richness that her struggles ceased. Instead she
put up her hands to encircle his neck, to revel in the
strength of this powerful man who, at that moment,
thought only of her, and she wriggled her body closer,
more closely still, so that they were moulded together.
Then time ceased to matter. Nothing mattered any more.
All that had ever happened had only been leading up to
this. This was what Tania had waited for all her life—
to be in this man's arms, and it had been planned thus
from the beginning of time. She was not even aware of
where she was any longer. Only the sweet sensation of

love and warmth and all-encompassing fire filled her, and there was nothing in the world save that. Locked in each other's arms, the kisses growing and blending into a time-less number, each different, and better than the last, and his hands delighting her eager body, she was unaware of anything else—until Ben began to bark, loudly, desper-ately, and hurled himself against the front door in a frenzy to get out.

It took several moments for the intrusive sound to register, but when it did she heard Bryden mutter: 'What the——' and his hands moved, were taken away, and he turned. She was left trembling, surfacing slowly from another world where no time existed; then she was alone in the room. She could scarcely move, but she managed to stagger to the window-seat before her legs buckled, then looked out of the window to see Ben chasing after two scared children. She heard Bryden call him very firmly, and Ben hesitated, then turned back reluctantly. Dazed, hardly comprehending, aware only of her own feelings, Tania watched the scene. Of course she loved him: she knew that now. She knew now what the pang of agony had been at her first sight of Margo. Margo—who was very probably his mistress. The pain had been jealousy.

CHAPTER SEVEN

How blind she'd been! Tania snatched up her pad and pencil and went to the door before Bryden could come in again. What was it he had once said, timeless aeons ago? 'You're as safe as you want to be.' How easily she could forget that when he moved in on her, and she succumbed like a star-struck teenager. He was an experienced man who knew all the moves in the game while Tania knew very few.

He was coming up the steps. He paused, looked at her, face, eyes, knowing, seeing everything, knowing all about her. 'We'd better go,' she said. She couldn't meet his eyes. She clutched her sketch pad tightly and heard the pencil snap in two, then she ran down the steps and past him.

He caught her up. She heard him go back to slam the door first, then he walked fast, and caught her up, and said :

'I'm sorry, Tania.'

He, apologising? She didn't want that. 'What for?' she said fiercely. 'You don't need to. *Nothing* happened. Nothing.' She was marching on. She couldn't look at him. Her face felt as if it were on fire. If those boys hadn't come——

'I didn't intend——'

She whirled on him then. 'What didn't you intend? To try and make love to me? Well, you damned well nearly did. I—I don't want——' she swallowed. 'I have to sleep in my house at night, knowing you're there——'

'Look.' He caught her arm. 'Stop a moment—please.'
She stopped, and looked at him, and she felt a deep
shame at herself. 'You needn't worry——'

'Oh! You mean I'm safe in the Lodge? That's super.
You'll only rape me on neutral ground, like the
Grange——'

'I don't mean that at all.' Bryden ran his hands through
his hair. 'Don't twist my words. You'd got me so angry
I wanted to teach you a lesson.'

'You did that all right. You taught me several, in fact.
Did *you* learn them from Margo?'

'What?' he seemed incredulous. '*Margo?* You don't
think——'

'I don't think anything. I only know what I see.' She
pulled herself free and marched on towards her house,
now visible. Fumbling for her key in her jeans pocket,
she opened the door and went in. She flung the sketch
pad on the kitchen table and burst into tears.

He came in the room after her and took her in his
arms. 'Don't cry,' he said. 'Oh God, don't weep——'

'I'm not. I'm——' she sniffed. 'J-just leave me *alone*!'

'Not when you're upset. You're safe, Tania, safe now.'
She was too. This embrace was a world away from what
had happened at the Grange. There was no passion in it,
merely a caring, a gentleness on his part that came to
her in his touch, and she relaxed, and whispered:

'It's all right—please, I'll be all right.'

'You're sure?' He stood back slightly, his face softened
by the look in his eyes, but still he held her, easily, com-
fortingly, and she nodded. What kind of fool must he
think her? She shuddered to think. It was time to salvage
the last remnants of her pride before he thought her a
complete child.

'I'll go and wash my face,' she said. 'And I'll get the plates out. You'd better go or even the fish and chip shop will be shut.'

He looked at her as if seeking some reassurance. 'Yes, I'm on my way. I'll get you something, okay?'

'Yes. Anything.'

He turned and went out without another word and a few moments later Tania heard his car pass the Lodge. She sat down at the table, and her mind was a confused jumble of thoughts and emotions, the most shattering of which was the knowledge that she was in love with him. She didn't know that that was how it happened, because it had never happened before. She hadn't realised that it was painful and wonderful and totally overwhelming, all at the same time.

She was still sitting there half an hour later when Bryden returned. She heard the car door slam and jumped out of the half dreamlike state guiltily, and ran to the plate cupboard. She hadn't been aware of time passing, and her cheeks flamed when he came in and saw her putting the plates out.

'Fish, chips and peas twice,' he said. 'That suit you?'

'Fine. Are you—er—working at the Grange this afternoon?'

'Probably. Why do you ask?'

'A friend might be coming around, that's all. Is it all right if I take her up there?'

'Sure. Someone from the village?'

'Yes.'

He nodded. 'As long as she's not a friend of Jack Latham's.'

'She's not. Her husband works for him, though.'

'Does he now?' He raised one eyebrow. 'And will *he* be coming with her?'

'Oh, I doubt it. He's very nice—I mean, he's not——'
Tania paused, floundering.

'I know what you mean. After all, there can't *be* many
like him, can there? Take her up by all means.'

The telephone shrilled in the hall, and Tania put her
knife and fork down and went to answer it. It was a
man, asking for Bryden.

She called him, and went back to finish her meal. She
could hear his voice through the half closed door quite
clearly, without having to try and listen. In fact it was
hard not to. And it was clear almost immediately that
the call concerned the Grange—and also Jack Latham.

She waited for him to finish. If he wanted to tell her,
he would. But she wasn't going to ask. She heard his
goodbye, the ding as the telephone receiver was replaced,
then he came back in.

'That was the solicitor,' he said. 'He's been trying to
get me all morning.'

'Oh.'

'Jack Latham phoned him yesterday. He's going down
to London on Monday to see him. Philip—the solicitor—
says he's out to cause trouble. I told him I already knew
that.'

'But what can he do?'

'Not much. But he's going to try. He wants the Grange
very badly—and even more now that he knows someone
else wants it. Philip thinks he's going to try blackmail.
Did you know he'd bought six acres adjoining these
grounds?'

'No, of course not,' she said.

'Neither did I. But he has. It looks very much to me as
though he'll be pulling all the stops out to get permission
for something on that land that will prove such a
nuisance that life at the Grange would be difficult.'

'Such as what?'

He shrugged. 'You tell me. He probably bought the land cheaply a while back, and he's just been biding his time. I'd like to know what's going on in his mind right now.'

'You mean he'd have something very noisy—like a night club?'

'Probably worse. A factory—I don't know. We might find out next week.'

Her eyes widened. 'But what can you do?'

He looked at her grimly. 'I'll find out first, then act.'

'Shouldn't you phone Mr Temple and tell him?'

'Philip will have already done so. But he's leaving it to me, anyway.'

'It's a lot of responsibility for you,' observed Tania.

'I know. It's also a challenge. And I haven't even begun to fight yet—but Jack Latham doesn't know that.' Bryden stood up. 'He's not seen me in action—but he will.'

Lunch was over, the house was quiet, and Bryden had gone back to the Grange to work. Tania was waiting for Beth. She desperately needed someone to talk to, if only to sort out the muddle in her brain. Too much was happening all at once. She felt as if someone had sandbagged her. Please hurry, she said inwardly. Beth closed the café after lunch on a Saturday and reopened on Monday for the twice weekly market trade. She drove her own small yellow Citroën, which she called, affectionately, the Flying Custard—and it was this which Tania was looking for when she heard a cheerful horn blast outside the front door. She rushed to open it, to see, instead of the Citroën, Jim's blue van. Then Beth emerged from the passenger side, waving.

'Hello, Tania, Jim decided to bring me.'

'Lovely!' Tania smiled warmly at the tall powerfully built figure who uncurled himself from behind the steering wheel. She wouldn't be able to talk now—but she was fond of Jim, who had an outrageous sense of humour and was guaranteed to get everyone laughing in any gathering. She hugged them both, and Jim grinned down at her.

'I've come to see this fellow that's managed to cause so much trouble in such a short time,' he said.

'Oh, I see, you've not come to see me,' she said severely. 'Serve you right if I don't take you to the Grange, then. Come on in, both of you, and we'll have a cup of coffee.'

They followed her in and Jim made straight for the lounge and sat down to talk to Ben, who always made a fuss of him. 'You can bring mine in here,' he said, 'when you've had your gossip. I know you women.'

Beth pulled a face at him and followed Tania out. 'Cheeky devil, he's only being nosey, you know. I told him he'd cop it from old Latham if he knew he'd been here and I can't possibly tell you what he answered to *that*, 'cos I'm too much of a lady.'

Tania laughed. 'I can guess.' She put the kettle on. 'I did want to talk to you, but perhaps later on.'

'Problems?'

'Too many. I wouldn't know where to start, Beth.'

'Oh *dear*!' Beth sat down, eyes full of concern. 'Since *he* came, I take it?'

'Mmm—more or less. What do I mean, more or less? Every damn thing has happened since he arrived.'

'Including the fact that you've rather fallen for him,' Beth said softly, and Tania nearly dropped the jar of coffee.

'*What!*'

'Sorry—sorry, my mistake.' But her eyes held the knowledge.

Tania nodded. 'How—how did you *know*? You've not even seen him——'

'You spoke about him, remember? Yesterday——'

'But I—didn't even know myself then!' Tania gaped at her friend.

'Didn't you?' Beth smiled.

Tania sat down suddenly, and Beth took the coffee jar out of her nerveless fingers and clucked. 'I'd better make that coffee. You're a bit useless at the moment.' She bustled about, quick and efficient, three cups of coffee no problem at all to her, used as she was to making enough for twelve or more in one go.

'You're a dark horse, Beth,' Tania said at last, when she clutched her beaker. 'No wonder you wanted to come here today! You're as nosey as Jim.'

'True, but for a different reason.' Beth smiled complacently. 'I know you too well, love, after all this time. There's not much you can hide from me.' She walked out with Jim's coffee and Tania heard her telling him to stay exactly where he was and talk to Ben. The door to the lounge was closed firmly, and Beth was back. 'Now,' she said, 'you'd better tell me *all*.'

'I think you already know most of it,' Tania said dryly, 'but here goes——'

She told of Margo's visit, and her own reactions, and of the work she was doing. She didn't venture in more personal matters; she couldn't talk about them to anyone. When she had finished Beth sighed.

'Hmm, well, one thing I'm quite sure of from what you've told me—this Bryden sounds a fascinating man, he really does.'

'You'll see for yourself quite soon. I told him I'd a

friend coming and would it be all right to show her the Grange—I didn't know Jim was bringing you then—and he said fine. He certainly won't mind Jim going too.' And in fact, she wondered what Jim would make of Bryden. A man's opinion of another man was usually different from a woman's. She smiled to herself. One thing was sure—Beth would tell her. Though why it should be so important to know puzzled her. After all, there was Margo. Beth hadn't met Margo, hadn't seen how glamorous and attractive she was. . . .

'Sorry? What did you say, Beth?'

'I said—when are we going?'

'Oh, we'll walk up now. Ever been in the Grange?'

'No, but I've always wanted to. I can't wait.'

'Right. We'll take Ben. Just let me make sure everything's locked up.' Tania checked that the back door was bolted, the cooker off, and they went to tell Jim.

The stroll up to the Grange was always pleasant, and never more so than on a fine summer's day with the sun gilding the leaves on the trees and a slight breeze rustling them so that the shadows danced. Beth looked round her. 'Oh, I love trees,' she said. 'That's what I miss, living in the village, you know.'

'I'll plant you one in the back yard, love,' grinned Jim, 'then you can stare at it all day——'

'Oh, shut up,' she hit his arm, but with affection. 'You know what I mean!'

'Nearly there,' said Tania. 'That's his car. Now do you wonder I thought he was a gipsy?'

'It's probably all he can afford,' said Beth. 'Anyway, it's the man that counts, not the car. Look at old Latham in his big Mercedes—huh!'

'You're speaking of the man who provides us with all

those little extras that make life worth living,' answered Jim. 'Though there are times——' he stopped, and grinned. 'No, not in front of ladies!'

'Hmm, I wonder what he was going to say?' laughed Beth. 'I can't imagine, can you, Tania?'

'No.' She laughed with them, but it wasn't funny, really. Jack Latham was a hard man to work for. Jim was independent-minded, but jobs were hard to come by locally, and as both he and Beth had elderly parents living in the village, neither wanted to move far away.

She ran up the steps and called. 'Bryden? Can we come in?'

Hammering stopped. He appeared at the top of the stairs, and Tania saw Beth looking upwards, and she wondered. . . .

'Surely.' He began to walk towards them, down the stairs. 'Excuse the dirt. Do come in.'

'These are my friends Beth and Jim Todd. Beth, Jim—Bryden Kane.' Bryden wiped his right hand down his jeans before shaking their hands.

'How d'you do. If you'd like to look round with Tania, you're very welcome, but I must warn you I've been ripping up a few floorboards upstairs. So be careful how you go.'

'Dry rot?' enquired Jim.

'The wood's in a bad state, certainly, but there's no smell of it—do you know anything about dry rot, Mr Todd? I'm no expert, I confess, but I'm getting them in next week.'

'Call me Jim. I do know something—shall I have a look?'

'I'd be delighted. Upstairs.' The two men ran up, leaving the two women in the hall. Beth looked at Tania, and Tania looked at Beth, but they said nothing until the two had vanished. Then Beth went: 'Phew!'

Tania pulled her arm and led her into the dining room. 'And what does that mean?' she whispered.

'Mmm, he is really very dishy,' whispered back Beth. 'Big as Jim—no, bigger. Cor!'

Tania laughed. 'You are funny!' Then, sobering, 'I don't know why I'm laughing. You haven't seen his girl-friend. Or one of them.'

'Cheer up. You're here—she isn't. Out of sight out of mind, remember.'

'Mmm—and absence makes the heart grow fonder!'

'Don't let's get on to the clichés!' Beth begged. 'Any-way, I don't care how gorgeous *she* is—you're quite something yourself, don't forget. Jim says if I ever left him he'd be after you like a shot!'

'Jim's a love,' Tania smiled. Then she sighed. 'Never mind. I'm not going to start moaning about me. Why should I? Men! Huh!' she tossed her mane of glorious copper-coloured hair. 'Let's go and look round, shall we?'

'Let's go and see what they're up to first. Did you see them wandering off as if they'd known each other for years? I want to know what they're talking about. We'll creep up very quietly and see.'

They did, followed by Ben, but they realised when they got upstairs that it wouldn't have mattered if they'd gone up banging drums for all the notice the two men took. Both were deep in conversation at the end of the corridor, looking out of the window that looked over the gardens, backs to the two women, something very serious about their stance, so much so that Beth caught Tania's arm.

'Wait,' she whispered. Silently they went into a front

bedroom, and Beth looked at Tania. Her expression was very curious, and Tania frowned.

'What is it?' she asked quietly.

'Did you see the way they were talking? They weren't even aware of us.'

'What do you think they're talking about?'

'I don't know,' Beth answered. 'But I've got a very strange feeling——' she stopped and looked at Tania.

Then Tania guessed. She nodded slowly. 'You think —Bryden's asking Jim to work for him?'

'I wouldn't be at all surprised.'

'But he wouldn't leave Latham, would he?'

'I don't know. I just don't know. But I'll bet my last tenpenny piece that that's what the talk's about.'

Beth shuddered. 'It's impossible. He'd have to say no. We live in the village, remember?'

'Yes, I know. Anyway, we're probably wrong. They're discussing the merits of football—or cars—or women.'

Beth gave a wry smile. 'I hope so. Let's go and see.' They walked along the corridor, assuming, both of them, airs of innocence as if it was quite normal for them to be there. 'Admiring the garden?' Beth enquired. 'I do love those trees. What a view!'

Both men looked round. Jim's face had changed; he wasn't smiling, which was rare. He usually was, especially in his wife's company. They were very close.

'Seen round?' he asked.

'Not yet.' Beth looked at him. 'Have you sorted out the wood problem?'

'Yes. There's no dry rot. The house seems sound. But some of the floorboards are shaky, due to age.' He looked at Bryden. 'I'm going to have to tell her.'

'Of course,' Bryden nodded. 'I wouldn't expect otherwise. You'll have to talk it over.'

Beth was looking from her husband to Bryden. Tania stood back and watched all three because she knew, at that moment, that what was going to be said didn't concern her. 'I think we'd better go downstairs, love,' Jim said to Beth.

'Shall Tania and I leave you?' Bryden asked.

Jim smiled. 'No. Not yet anyway. It's this, Beth. Bryden has asked me if I'd like to come and work here for several months, and I like the idea, but I said I'd talk it over with you——'

'You can't!' Beth looked at Bryden. 'I'm sure you mean well, Mr Kane, but after the work's finished, what then? Do you think Latham would welcome him back with open arms? Because I'll tell you the answer to that. He won't.'

'I know, Mrs Todd.' Bryden's eyes on her were very serious. 'And that's also something we've been talking over. Jim's ideal for here, I know that—but I appreciate your problems. But there's a possibility of something else, after the work here's finished. Unfortunately it's not quite clear yet—but I'm working on it.'

'I think I'd better go,' Tania began. 'This is really nothing to do——'

'No, Tania, I'd like you to stay.' Jim spoke, and he looked at Beth as he did so. 'You might help to make Beth see what I'm getting at——'

'I *know* what you're getting at. You want to work here with Mr Kane. And that would be lovely if you didn't work for Latham, but you do—and I also have a café to run, remember?' Beth stared at Bryden. 'I'd find all my customers vanishing. I know Latham, you don't.'

He smiled. 'Oh, but I do. We had a very unpleasant scene in Tania's house the other night in which he threatened to get me out by fair means or foul. I don't take kindly to threats and I didn't like him at all. I appreciate that as a stranger here I'm not in the same position as you, and that you actually live in the village —but the owner of this house has one or two tricks up his sleeve that I can't tell you about—yet. I do assure you, though, that Mr Latham will soon not be in any position to blackmail you or anyone else who wants to work for me here.'

'Fine words!' Beth laughed. 'How do you guarantee that?' The laughter died as she saw what was on Bryden's face, and even Tania felt herself grow colder, as if a chill had entered the house.

'Mrs Todd, would you and Jim like to come back to the Lodge with me? And then, with Tania's permission, I'm going to make a phone call.' He looked at Tania. 'It's long distance, I'm afraid, but I'll do it the usual way.'

She nodded, unable to speak. He looked at Jim. 'Shall we go? You can see round afterwards, when you've heard all I have to say.'

'Mr Kane, do we have much choice?' asked Beth, bemused.

He laughed, and the brief tension, the fear, that had entered Tania's mind, was dispelled. There had been such a force in his words, so hard, yet so softly said——

'I promise you, hand on heart, Mrs Todd, that I am not an ogre. Forgive me if I've given you that impression. It most certainly was not my intention.' His smile was on her, his eyes, those startlingly blue eyes, were almost gentle. Tania could see Beth almost visibly melting.

'Well——' she said, and Jim took her arm.

'Come on. Tania, can we cadge another cup of your delicious coffee?'

Tania nodded. Jim and Beth walked on ahead and she was left with Bryden. She looked at him and shook her head.

'I'm going crazy—I think,' she said.

'You're not, and neither am I.' Beth and Jim were out of sight. Ben waited patiently. 'He's a good man. I like him. I want him working here.'

'And you usually get what you want? You haven't known Beth for long, though, have you?'

He grinned. 'No.'

'She's a mind of her own.'

'I see that. I like her too.'

Tania laughed and began walking away. 'So do I. I like them both.' She paused, sobered. 'And I don't want them hurt. You'll soon be gone, remember that.'

Bryden was beside her, his arm almost touching hers, very big, very strong.

'They won't be hurt, I promise you that,' he said quietly.

'You can't promise——'

'You don't know what I can do. Not yet. But you will.'

Tania recalled those words later when, back at the Lodge, Bryden had gone upstairs to telephone from her bedroom extension. It had been Tania's suggestion, to give him more privacy and to enable Beth and Jim to talk. She made an excuse and went into the kitchen, leaving the two of them with a lot to say to each other in the lounge, and she stood at the window looking out at her small sunny garden, and she seemed to hear his words again. 'You don't know what I can do. Not yet.

But you will.' What was it about those perfectly harm-less words that had so filled her with a kind of in-evitability? It was as if he could sweep people along on a tide of softly spoken words, as if—she shivered—she had never met a man like him before. No bluff and bluster, nothing save those eyes which could become like steel, and his face—she remembered his face as he had spoken. There was such an inner strength there that for a moment she feared for anyone who dared oppose him. Jack Latham didn't know what he was up against.

Bryden had been gone for a quarter of an hour when she heard him coming down the stairs and hastily put the kettle on. He came straight into the kitchen and she turned: 'They're talking—I thought I'd leave them for a while.'

'Yes, so I gathered. I'll have my coffee out here. I need one.' He sat down.

'How did your calls go?' asked Tania.

He smiled faintly. 'Well enough. Do you mind if I don't tell you until we're all together? It saves repetition.'

'Look,' she said, 'it's nothing to do with me any-way——'

'They're your friends. You're part of it. Unless you don't want to be?'

She shrugged. 'I know Jim would be ideal to work on the Grange. He's one of those men who can do practically anything and do it well. Plastering, brickwork, glazing, decorating—he takes a pride in his work too. You should see their café and their home above it. He converted it from a near-derelict shop. So as far as work goes, you'll not get much better, but they each have a mother living in the village—they can't just leave, even if they wanted to, afterwards.'

'I know. Jim told me that. I appreciate it.' He looked up at her as she handed him a beakerful of coffee. 'Thanks.'

'And in any case, I'm already part of it, whether I want to be or not. It's my fault for introducing you——'

'Fault? Do you feel guilty?'

'No. You don't understand——'

'Oh, but I do. I'll tell you something, Tania. Jim told me he really wanted to meet me. He's already heard something of Latham's fury over the Grange. He wanted to see what I was like, to warn me, if necessary, what I was up against. He doesn't like bully boys any more than I do—we talked, we said quite a lot before you came up those stairs. And we've a lot more to say.'

Tania sat down very slowly. 'Oh,' she said, and he smiled.

'Shall we go in?'

'Yes. I'll make their coffee.'

They carried two each in, and Beth and Jim were talking earnestly in the lounge as they entered.

'Well,' said Beth, 'we've been talking. I can tell you now, Mr Kane——'

'Bryden, please——'

'Bryden, that you're a very clever and persuasive man. Jim's almost convinced me that working here would be the best thing he could do. But I've got more sense than him. I think about afterwards as well. He can't convince me on that. Let's see if you can.'

Tania hid a smile. Bryden might be able to quell opposition when it came in male form. But Beth was a very determined woman. He might have met his match here.

'Beth—may I call you Beth?—I'm not sure if you meant the clever and persuasive bit as a compliment or not, but I'll take it as one anyway. But I'm not going to cause friction between man and wife. I'd like you, though, to listen to what I have to tell you as a result of my phone call. First, I'd like your word, both of you, that this is all in strict confidence?'

'Of course. That goes without saying,' Jim answered, and Beth nodded.

'Right. Are we all sitting comfortably?' Bryden looked around at them, and Tania was aware of the subtle shift of emphasis in the room. The focus was on him, and it was what he intended. He alone remained standing, holding his coffee, looking at Beth and Jim seated on the settee.

'I telephoned the owner's solicitor at home. He's an old friend of John Temple's—the owner of the Grange. I also know him very well. I told him that I'd met someone who would be ideal for work here and explained some of the difficulties attendant on you, Jim, leaving Latham and coming to work here. He then told me something which I already knew partly but needed confirmation of—and this is the confidential part. Jack Latham's business activities are under investigation by a team of enquiry agents. They've already found out quite a lot about him, and I've been assured there's more—much more—to come. Philip—the solicitor—assured me that when the investigation is finished, and there's a way to go yet, our friend Jack Latham will be in no position to make life difficult for anyone.'

'What you are saying is that he's a crook?' said Beth.

Bryden smiled slightly. 'Let's say that they've already found out that he got one very lucrative contract for building a school by greasing a few palms and having access to quotations from other firms so that he knew precisely how much to tender in advance. Now he's also got quite a few local councillors in his pocket. I could name names, but I won't—yet. I don't know them personally, you might do. If and when necessary, I will.' He paused. 'Now, the other worry of yours, Beth, and you too, Jim. What happens when the work here is over? You can't, as Beth pointed out very logically, go back to Latham and tell him you'd like your job back. And this is where I come to the most important reason for my call. It was to check something I needed to know. The new owner of the Grange intends to spend some of his vast fortune on something that will be of benefit to everyone —namely a hospital. The nearest is York. He's already been into this thoroughly, apparently, and there's a crying need for one in this area. There'll be work on that for you, Jim, and if you do everything as well as I expect here, you'll find it a job of some importance—and very well paid. It will be a private hospital, nothing to do with the National Health—but with free beds for those needing them. There's a huge trust fund involved here worth millions. The job will take several years. And after that——' he shrugged. 'Who knows? There'll be more. Now, what do you say?'

Jim and Beth looked at each other. Tania saw her nod, almost imperceptible, but she knew—and so did Jim. 'Right,' he said. 'When do I start?' He stood up and went over to Bryden and they shook hands. 'I'd like to meet my new boss,' Jim said. 'He sounds a good man.'

'You will,' Bryden answered. 'That's the other thing. John Temple is coming here next week.' He smiled. 'It'll be a flying visit—literally. He's coming by helicopter on Thursday.'

CHAPTER EIGHT

You could have heard a pin drop, thought Tania. For a few moments, after Bryden's words, there was a startling silence, broken at last by Beth.

'My God, you're a quick worker as well, aren't you?'

'Yes, in some ways I am.' He smiled at her.

'And full of surprises. I take it the hospital is confidential too?'

'Yes, very.'

'Well, I think it's a good idea. I hope I'll meet your Mr Temple on Thursday? I'd like to.'

'Of course. Now, Jim, shall we go back to the Grange and discuss practical matters?'

'I'd like that.' Jim stood up. He looked slightly dazed, as if what was happening was too much to take in all at once. Tania knew the feeling well. She had had two days to get accustomed to it, Jim hadn't.

'We'll stay here,' said Beth. 'I've a feeling I'm going to see quite a bit of the Grange in the near future. I'd rather sit here—I'm not sure if I can stand, to be quite honest.'

Jim bent to kiss her. 'See you later,' he said. 'Look after her, Tania, she's a fragile little lass. After you, Bryden.' The two men went out, and Tania could hear their laughter as they set off walking, but this time she knew why, and it was all right.

'Phew, what a man!' said Beth in heartfelt tones. 'He's like a human bulldozer.'

'Something like that,' Tania agreed.

'I can see why you've fallen. He's quite irresistible, isn't he?'

'Don't let Jim hear you!'

'No, you know what I mean! He is a very attractive fellow, but you don't need me to tell you that. I think I need another coffee. Can I——?'

'I'll do it. Stay here, won't be a moment.'

Tania hurried out to make it. She herself needed a drink, after all the shocks, but it seemed for the moment as if she had to be the strong one. Beth's whole life was going to change, and just because of a casual visit. Hers would go back to being the same soon—when Bryden had gone. She nearly dropped a cup, and put it down carefully. When he had gone—she felt a wave of depression sweep through her. There would come that day, it was inevitable, when Bryden Kane would no longer be there. She wondered if she would be able to bear it. A day when he would pack up and go, leaving the house ready for John Temple, and he would say goodbye, and that would be that. And life would never be quite the same again. He might even marry Margo, and visit his brother-in-law, and, it was just possible, call in to say hello. Only I won't be here, she thought. She knew that it was inevitable. She would go. Soon, when the Grange was finished, she would leave. The Lodge had never really belonged to her any more than it had to her grandfather. Tania saved carefully, and had a neat bank balance, nothing startling, but enough to find her a place somewhere away from here.

She wondered why the kitchen had suddenly become blurred, and blinked hard and sniffed. 'Don't be stupid,' she told herself fiercely. She decided in advance that she wouldn't really like John Temple, which she knew was unfair. He had saved—or was about to save—the Grange from being destroyed. And nothing could be worse than that. But he was also a jet-setter, a playboy, however traditional his tastes in home or furniture, and Tania could imagine only too well the kind of friends he would have visiting. It would never be the same as the old days. She had already met Margo, any impartiality of judgment being impossible because of her relationship with Bryden. Tania paused for a moment. There was a point. If she had met Margo without Bryden being on the scene, what would she have thought about her? She was not what Tania imagined a member of the jet set to be. Neither brash nor arrogant, she had in fact been pleasant and warm—almost friendly, in fact. Perhaps a miracle would happen and John Temple would also be charming. She sighed; she would soon know.

Beth looked at her when she went in. 'Thank goodness! I thought you'd got lost!'

'I notice you didn't rush out to see,' Tania answered, smiling.

'Couldn't. I'm just getting over all the surprises.'

'Mmm, I know what you mean. You're getting some idea of what's hit *me*.' She sat down beside Beth on the settee. 'I was just wondering what J.T. would be like,' she added.

'Oh, *him*? The new owner?' Beth nodded. 'So was I. He must be a millionaire, Tania. Just think—a *millionaire*! I've never met one.'

'Neither have I.'

'I wonder if he's good-looking. How old did Bryden say he is?'

'Um—I got the impression late thirties——'

'What if he falls for you?' Beth's eyes widened. 'Just imagine! Play your cards right and you could end up as mistress of the Grange.'

'Mistress is probably the right word—they marry their own kind. No, thanks, I'll stay independent. Anyway, he probably won't even notice me, except as the nuisance who's living in his lodge. I'm not staying, Beth. When he moves in—when Bryden's gone—I'm moving out.'

Beth gave a little shriek. 'You're *not*! You *can't*——'

'I can. I've thought about it, and it's the only logical thing. Living here is fine now, with the Grange empty. It's really all mine, and I do love it here, but, when he's living there, it could never be the same. And Latham could make my job difficult. I know Bryden's said they're finding out about him, but there are still small ways he can get back at me—plus the fact that I've finished with Ted. He won't forgive that in a hurry, remember.'

Beth sighed. 'I know. It seems such a *shame*, that's all. I hope you don't move too far away, though—I'd miss you.'

'Of course I won't! I was brought up here, virtually, and you've always been such a close friend—we'll sort something out, you'll see.'

'Of course we will.' They sat drinking their coffee without speaking for several minutes, each engrossed in thought. Tania's were now becoming clearer. The decision had been made. She would start looking in the newspapers from now on to get an idea of what kind of teaching posts were available, and where. There would be no immediate rush, but the sooner she began to plan, the better. She'd have to find an apartment which welcomed animals, because Ben was an important consideration. Perhaps even a small house, with a garden. . . .

'Oh, it's a funny world, isn't it?' Beth's words broke the silence.

'Mmm, you can say *that* again,' agreed Tania. 'Look,

you and Jim stay to tea—please—there's salad in the fridge, and I can make a trifle in five minutes——'

'You've convinced me! Let me phone home to check the kids are all right. They knew we were coming but I didn't know we'd be long. It was honestly just a flying visit——'

'Fine. Of course.' Beth had two daughters, Ruth and Jane, twins of fourteen, besides Tony, and had left them at home with their brother. She went to telephone while Tania began to look out the trifle ingredients. Tania heard her voice faintly, then an exclamation, a few more words, and the telephone was replaced.

'Hell's bells!' Beth never swore, which was why Tania whirled round on hearing such alien words.

'What?'

'You'll never guess! Latham phoned, wanting a word with Jim—and guess what? Our dear daughter Jane answered and told him we'd come here!'

'Oh!' Tania stared in dismay at her friend. 'Oh dear. Jane wouldn't know, of course. You can't blame her——'

'No, of course not. The child was being helpful. But just imagine! He knows *we're* friends, but you can bet he's wondering what Jim's doing here as well. He'll very probably think the worst.'

'Which won't be far from the point. You'd better tell Jim when he gets back here. At least it'll prepare him.'

'But I wonder what he *wanted?*' Beth mused, puzzled. 'It's practically unheard-of for him to telephone.'

'He could have passed here, seen his van and decided to check up. And don't forget, he could think you were both visiting me, which, in a sense, you are.'

'Mmm. We'll soon find out anyway. There's one thing about Latham, he doesn't waste time letting you know if he's annoyed about something!'

Both men returned shortly afterwards; it was clear they had both done a lot of talking—and working. Both were dusty and perspiring and in no fit state to sit at a table. Beth and Tania looked them, then at each other.

'What on earth have you been doing?' gasped Beth.

Jim had the grace to look sheepish; Bryden merely grinned. 'We got to checking on some cupboards,' said Jim, 'and one thing led to another. They needed ripping out—so we did.'

'So it looks too! I think you'd both better go and have a good wash.'

Bryden saluted crisply, 'Yes, ma'am.' And all four burst out laughing, while Beth went a bright pink.

'Oh—I didn't mean——' she gasped——

'It's okay, you're quite right. We're both filthy.' He looked at Jim. 'It seems you've already started work, Jim. Your salary had better commence from today. I'll see to it.'

'I've got a week's notice to work first,' Jim answered.

'Maybe you won't have,' said Beth. 'Latham phoned, and Jane told him you were here.'

'Did he now? I wonder what he wanted?' Jim frowned. 'That's unusual. Can I call him from here, Tania?'

'Feel free. Don't let it ruin your tea—he may sack you.'

'It won't. I'll go and wash first if I may, then phone.'

'I'll get you a clean towel.' He followed Tania out.

Several minutes later, while Bryden had gone up to clean the dirt off, Jim telephoned his employer, and the two women prepared the meal. He was on the telephone for quite a few minutes, then they heard it go down, and he walked back in.

'The old b——' he visibly checked himself, and sat down. 'He knew I was here—he finds out everything, one way or another. And he had the nerve to demand the reason!' He was smouldering, that much was obvious.

'And?' Beth queried, wide-eyed.

'So I told him, didn't I? The phone nearly exploded. He's threatened me with just about everything he can— he was *mad*, I can tell you that. So I told him what he could do with County Construction and hung up.' He looked at Tania. 'It seems I'll be starting work here sooner than I thought.'

Beth sat down. 'Oh dear! It's all my fault.'

'Why?' he asked.

'Well, I told you about Bry——' she stopped as Bryden walked in, and Jim looked at him.

'I'm a free man, as from this moment. I just told my ex-boss what he could do with his job. Do I start on Monday?'

'You do. Nine o'clock at the Grange? Now, Jim, do you know of any others who'd be willing to work for us here? I mean good, reliable men who're not afraid of hard work.'

'Several. But they're all Latham's men.'

'Can you talk to them? Before he gets to them, I mean. You can be damned sure he'll be phoning round to make sure no one else does what you just did.'

'I don't know. How many do you need?'

'At least four more. Especially those with plumbing and electrical expertise.'

'I've got a few in mind. Tania, can we use your phone again?'

'Sure.' She looked at Beth helplessly, and Beth grinned.

'I'll pay your next phone bill,' said Bryden. 'Let's start now. Eat your tea. We'll have ours later.' They went into the hall and closed the door.

'Well, there's one thing about salad,' Beth remarked. 'It can't get cold and spoil.'

And they began to eat.

It was late evening and growing dusk as Tania took Ben out for his last walk of the day. It had been a tiring day. Beth and Jim had left an hour or so previously after much more talking. Bryden was working in the kitchen, and Tania needed to get away and think. She needed to be alone for a while. So many things were happening all at once that she wondered if life would ever resume its calm, even tenor again. It seemed incredible that one man could have brought so much disruption into her life, and the lives of others, but he had.

Now, walking through the trees in the cool half light of evening, she could think clearly for the first time in over twelve hours. Ben ambled on ahead, the perfect companion, no talk needed, and she followed. After Monday things would never be the same at the Grange. Work would begin, and the place would be alive with men during the days of the week. There would be vans and lorries arriving loaded with materials needed for the refurbishing of the beautiful old house, and she would be there, watching it happen, and it would be both happy and sad at the same time.

She had gone past the Grange, past the flat bowling green and ancient pavilion, past the disused tennis court, and was entering the thickly wooded area beyond the house, and all was quiet and still. Night held no fears for Tania. Little frightened her, for what was there to fear here? And Ben was with her. Bryden had offered to take Ben, but she had refused, explaining that she enjoyed her late evening walks alone. She thought of Ted, and of how things had gone so wrong. She hadn't wanted it to end like that. She didn't like hurting anyone, even though she had known all along that she would never love him enough to marry him.

Ben had vanished, and she waited, listening, and called him until he came running to her. 'Hey, you mustn't disappear like that,' she scolded, and he wagged his tail apologetically. She had been climbing a gentle rise, and when she emerged from the trees she could look down and see the Grange and its gardens spread out below her, and beyond, a glimpse of the Lodge roof and chimneys, and beyond that the ribbon of road winding into the village. The sky was dotted with stars, not many yet, but there soon would be, and a full moon drifted lazily along, keeping pace with her. She felt suddenly sad. She sat on a rock, Ben by her side, and gazed over the sleeping countryside, and wondered about life, and the reason for everything. She felt very much alone. She drew her jacket round her, thankful she had put it on, for the night was cool, and she saw Bryden's face, and loving him hurt. It wasn't nice, being in love. It was painful, an empty aching and a longing, and it would be so much easier if she could just see him as a man, an ordinary man who was there to work for his employer. And that would never be possible, not now. For Bryden had awakened responses in her that she had not imagined could exist. He had aroused a love in her that was overwhelming. To him she was what? Just another woman he met on his travels? He had told her he was a wanderer, a jack of all trades—she tried to smile to herself. He underestimated himself. There was nothing of the casual wanderer about him. Perhaps he had already set his sights on a target: Margo. He'd played it cool with her all right—Tania's heart ached at the memory of them together. Both so tall, Margo elegant, Bryden rougher, tougher, but somehow they looked right together. They matched. They were two of a kind. He was a very clever man, was Bryden. And I nearly succumbed, she thought in faint horror. It wouldn't have take much more....

'Tania!' A faint voice drifted up, and Ben barked. Tania hushed him instantly, but it was too late.

'Go away!' she whispered. She didn't want him; she wanted to be alone for a while longer, to sort out her thoughts.

'Tania? Where are you?' The voice was nearer now, and she could hear the crackling of twigs, almost charting his progress as he climbed steadily. He must have heard Ben's brief response.

She stood up. He'd find her anyway. 'I'm here.'

'Are you all right?'

'Of course I am,' she answered. What on earth did he mean? She saw his tall shadowy figure emerge from the trees, blurred by the growing darkness, and her heart ached with all the pent-up longing she didn't understand, and wasn't sure if she wanted to.

She waited for him to reach her; she could have gone down to meet him, but it seemed right for her to stand there and wait. He looked up as he approached. She couldn't see the expression on his face, whether he was smiling or serious. 'You were sitting up here?' he said.

'Why not? It's a nice place to sit and think.'

'All right.' He walked towards the stone and sat down. Then he patted the space beside him.

'Alone,' she said, and he laughed.

'Look,' he said, 'I came to see if you were all right. You'd been gone so long——'

'So long? What do you mean? I'd been away about ten——'

'An hour is more like.' Tania looked at her watch in disbelief, catching the light from the moon on the face of it, briefly; shocked to see that indeed an hour had passed since she had left the Lodge.

'Oh.' She sat down. 'And you were worried?'

'I wondered where you'd got to. What were you thinking about?'

'It's been a busy day. Where would you like me to start?'

He laughed. 'It has rather. I've now got staff. One at least, definitely, and there'll be others.'

'I'm sure there will. Your Mr Temple knew what he was doing when he picked you, didn't he?'

'He's a very wealthy man. He can afford the best.'

'And you are. The best, I mean?'

He shrugged. 'Modesty forbids.'

'Oh, come on! Modest, you are not.'

'True.' He sighed a little sigh. 'How well you see through me, Tania.'

She started to move, prepared to stand. It was time to go. She didn't want to be sitting here with him, like this —then he caught her arm. 'Wait.'

'Why? It's late—you told me——'

'I didn't say that. I said you'd been gone an hour.' He looked at her. 'There's a difference. An hour out, alone, at this time of night, for you, a woman—anything could happen. But I'm here.'

'Yes, I know. *That* makes a difference?'

'At least no one will attack you.'

'They're not likely to anyway. No one ever comes here, not at night.'

'You don't know that. And now there's Latham——'

'Him? It's the Grange he's after, not me.'

'Don't be too sure. I don't like him, or his methods. I'd prefer if you didn't come so far away from your house alone at night in future—at least not until everything's sorted out.'

'Meaning?' she queried.

'Meaning simply that in a week or so things will have changed considerably. He won't be a threat to anybody then.'

'And until then you'd prefer me to stay closer to home?'

'Something like that.'

'Then I will. I'm not foolish. Although I don't imagine he has strong-arm boys——'

'Possibly not. Humour me, though. I'm responsible in a way for all the bother with Latham—and his son.'

'In a way,' she agreed dryly. 'You could say that.'

'Would you prefer to go back to things as they were?'

There was a brief silence. Tania heard the question echo and re-echo inside her head, and in the strangest way it was as if this was something she had been waiting to hear. And she knew the answer within her, and she had always known the answer to that particular question. No, oh no, there was no going back now, and never could be.

'That's an odd question,' she said. 'How can anything ever be as it was again?'

'That wasn't my question. I didn't say could it—I said would you prefer it?'

'Would I prefer knowing what was going to happen—what Latham intended for the Grange? Of course not.'

'But you wouldn't have known. Not for a while anyway.'

'It would still have happened. You stopped him—or rather John Temple did.'

'So I take it you would rather things were as they are now?'

'Why do you keep asking? Is it so important?'

Then something changed. Subtle, the change, but there. A heightening of the tension, so that her heart began to beat faster and she was drawn to look at him, as irresistibly as iron towards a magnet, and in the pale cool light of the moon she saw the different expression on his face. The air was very still, and shimmering with a kind of awareness that filled the night, and coloured everything with its own magic. Tania also was now very still, because to move would be to break the spell, and she waited for him to speak. She waited . . . she waited. . . .

'Yes,' he said, 'it is important.' She couldn't see his eyes, they were darker, shadowed, deep-set. But she could see the planes of his face, the bone structure, hard outline, square strong chin, mouth a blur—his voice was deeper, and slightly husky.

'Then—I suppose, yes,' she said hesitantly. 'To see the Grange being restored, to see it come to life again, will be very satisfying.'

'I was talking to Beth. She said that when it's done, you'll leave.'

'Yes. I thought I'd already told you.' Tania felt confused. 'It wouldn't be right for me to stay. I love this part of the world very much, I'd never go too far away—but the Lodge won't be the same when——' she hesitated.

'When the new owner moves into the Grange?' he prompted.

'Yes.'

'What about Ben?'

'What about him?'

'You'd have to find somewhere that will take a dog.'

'I know. You don't think I'd leave him behind, do you? Besides, John Temple may have a dog or dogs of his own. Ben's smashing, but he tends to be very proprietorial over what he considers *his* garden.' She shivered. 'I mean, he'd make mincemeat of, say, a couple of corgis.'

Bryden laughed. 'You have a point. I do know, however, that John Temple has a labrador bitch puppy— Ben certainly wouldn't cause problems there——' he paused. 'Mmm, I don't know, though——' he seemed very amused. It was definitely time to go.

Tania stood up, and this time he didn't stop her. 'I'm getting rather cold,' she said. 'I'd like to go back now.'

'Sure.' He stood up, unfurling his long length slowly, this big man who towered over her, was infinitely strong, threatening—because he made her feel so very vulnerable when he was near. And he was too near now. It was too dark to feel comfortable with him and she wished she didn't love him, because then, how much easier everything would be. . . .

Her whole body tingled with his nearness, so she moved away, began walking, and Ben, who had got bored and wandered off to sniff a few trees, reappeared. They began walking side by side in the darkness, only the moon to light their path, wending down towards the trees, and the Grange, and home. Bryden didn't speak, and Tania, who was never lost for words, couldn't. Because her heart was beating erratically, and she knew what it must be like to walk with a lover through the dark shadows of the night, and be safe and wanted, and for a few moments she allowed herself to fantasise that he loved her, and that they were going home together, to be together for always. . . .

She stumbled on a hidden tussock of grass and he caught her arm. They were near the trees now. 'Careful!' he said. The touch sent a shock pulsing up her arm to her shoulder and she wanted to pull away, but dared not. Surely he could hear the blood pounding in her head? It was like a roar of sound. Then he moved his hand, so that it was on her forearm, then he slid it down and clasped her fingers in his. 'This is safer,' he said. 'You need protecting.'

From you I do, she thought, but she couldn't take her hand away, and she didn't want to. She had held men's hands before, and that had been fun, on country walks, in the late evening perhaps, walking back from the village with a boy when she was younger. This wasn't fun, it was very different. Bryden's hand was warm and strong, but his clasp was gentle, and the little shock waves were dying down now, because the first impact had passed, but it was still the most wonderful thing in the world, ever.

'I'm all—right,' she managed to murmur, oh, so casually, as if it meant absolutely nothing. 'I'm a big girl now, you know.'

'Mmm, I know.' The words were double-edged, and his voice held the touch of laughter, yet not laughter, and she thought, I'll remember this all the rest of my life, which seemed an absurd thought to have, yet it was so. They were in the trees now, pitch darkness around them, Ben ambling ahead, sure of his way, and they followed. The branches and smaller twigs caught at them, and Bryden put up his free hand to hold, to brush them aside, but he didn't let go of her hand, not once.

Then he stopped. They were nearly out of the trees now, and it was still dark, although there was a glimmer of light ahead, and he tugged her hand and said:

'Ssh! Listen.'

Tania froze. 'What?'

'Can you hear anything?'

She strained her ears, but could hear nothing, save their breathing. 'No,' she whispered.

'It sounded like an animal scuttling through the undergrowth——'

'There'd be nothing. Only rabbits, and they'd keep out of Ben's way——'

'No, wait. There it is again——'

She felt the prickles of fear on the back of her neck at his tone, but she still couldn't hear a sound save them. Ben had vanished. He would be waiting at the Lodge gate, wondering where they had got to. 'Does it worry you?' she whispered.

'No. I like to know what things are, though. Don't you?'

'If I can hear them. I can't.'

'I'm going to the Grange. You go on home——'

'No, I'm coming with you!'

'All right. Come on.' They changed direction and came round by the back of the dark silent house, and Bryden went and tried the back door. It was locked.

'I'm going in,' he said.

'Why? If it was an animal——'

'It could have been someone moving.'

'Ben would have known. He'd have barked——

'Not necessarily. The breeze is blowing downwards. The noise was from behind.'

'I'm coming in with you,' she said.

'Aren't you frightened?'

'Are you?'

He laughed softly, searching for his key. 'No. Do I look it?'

'No.' She wasn't frightened, not with him there. He could deal with anybody, anything that ever happened. But she wouldn't tell him so.

He opened the door quietly and they went in, and he closed it softly behind them. They stood in the dark passage to the kitchen, and waited, listening. Tania's heart was thudding unbearably, but there was nothing she could do about it. Then, walking so carefully that they made no sound at all, they went forward. Bryden took her hand again. He had released her to open and close the door.

They stood in the hall, and the whole house was silent. Then they waited again, and if anyone had been in they would have heard something by now, because it was impossible for anyone to stand as silently as they did. Tania shivered slightly, and felt Bryden's arm go round her so that he held her. She looked up, to begin to tell him that no one else could possibly be there, and he looked down at her at the same moment, and she saw him smile faintly in the pale insubstantial light from the high landing windows. Then he bent his head, and the light was blotted out, and his lips found hers, so that what she had been going to say was lost for ever.

She hadn't wanted this to happen. She tried to tell herself that, in the innermost part of her mind as his hard, demanding mouth came down on hers, and she knew the thought was a lie, but it didn't matter now, because all she ever wanted was to be locked in his arms, and now she was. She knew she should be resisting, not just letting it happen, because Margo and he. . . .

But the struggles were no good, and only excited him more, she could sense that, and her whole body was afire with longing because that was the effect he had, and she hated her own treacherous response as she put her arms round him, lost now, uncaring. Margo wasn't here. . . . Margo would have him back, soon, but now, just for the moment, he was hers.

Then cold sanity returned, as in a flash of insight she knew the truth. There had not been any noise. Her ears were very keen, and yet she had heard nothing. Bryden had wanted to get her here, and had succeeded. And there could be only one reason for that, because here it was dark, and there were too many lights in the Lodge, and Ben there as well. Here, if. he wanted, and he did want, he could make love to her. . . .

'No!' She wrenched herself free, gasping for breath, ashamed at her own reaction. 'You—you——' She whirled away from him and ran unsteadily towards the front door and pulled it open. How blind she had been, and how clever he was!

He caught up with her. 'Be careful—it's too dark——'

'Don't touch me!' She knocked his restraining hand away and shouted the words at him, eyes blazing with temper. 'I *know* it's too dark—my God! You must think I'm a fool! Leave me alone—just leave me *alone*!' and she ran out and blindly down the steps, the tears blurring her eyes so that she couldn't see where she was going. The next moment she was sprawled headlong on the ground.

CHAPTER NINE

THE fall had knocked the breath from her. Dazed, she was aware of Bryden bending over her, and she opened her eyes to see his blurred face, white with shock, looking down at her. She tried to stand up, to escape him, to escape her treacherous love for him, and the world spun round with her effort. He picked her up and looked into her eyes. 'I'm going to carry you home,' he said.

'I don't *need* you—I can manage,' she gasped.

'No, you can't. Stay still. My God, why did you run like that? I wasn't going to——'

'I know what you were going to do,' she muttered, but she couldn't struggle, and didn't try. Bryden was walking swiftly with her towards the Lodge, and Ben came running up, puzzled.

He went in and put her down on the settee in the lounge before switching on the lights. Then he came over to her, and she glared up at him. 'I'm all right, I've not broken any bones. *Leave me alone!*'

The shock of her fall was passing. She wasn't hurt, only shaken from it. What had shaken her even more was her own desire for him. She had wanted him to make love to her, that was the awful, terrible thing, she now realised fully. And to him she would be a mere fleeting affair, no more. She had no illusions about that. 'You must think I'm a fool,' she said bitterly. 'There was no noise. You—you just wanted to get me to the Grange, and then——'

'And then—what? Rape you? In there?' He stood up, and ran his fingers through his dark hair. 'Thanks! Thanks very much. You won't believe me about the noise. Okay, I don't expect you to. I did hear something, I swear it. And I know what Latham would like to happen——'

'There was no one in there.'

'No, but I had to see. You insisted on going with me, remember?'

'Only because I didn't fancy walking alone——'

'Because you thought there was someone? Make up your mind. One minute I'm a liar——'

'You got me confused. You'd get anyone confused——' She glared at him, cheeks pink, hair tousled from her fall, and she saw his face change as he looked at her, but she didn't know why. She only knew that it made her heart beat faster. Her arm hurt where she had jarred it when she fell, and she rubbed it, and looked away from those eyes of his as she did so.

'Have you hurt your arm?'

'Yes.'

'Let me see.'

'No. You can't do anything. You've done enough——'

'Don't be childish, Tania. If it's hurt it needs attention. Now, let me see.'

He sat down on the settee and she moved her body back, away from him, with difficulty. The settee wasn't very big.

He helped her take off her jacket, then took hold of her right arm and looked at it. She wanted to scream out at his touch. She hated him. No, she didn't—'Oh!'

'There?'

'Yes. It's—my elbow——' She drew in her breath

sharply, as his hands moved very gently along her arm, but he wasn't hurting. His touch raised goose pimples on her skin; she shivered.

'I don't think you've broken any bones. You've had a bad jolt. Got anything to rub on?'

'Some ointment—it's in the kitchen——' she began to get up and he pushed her back.

'Let me. Just tell me where.'

She told him, he left, and she sat there, chagrined at her own impulsive rush to escape what had led to this. And he—what did he think, or care? He was probably trying not to laugh. He wouldn't fool her again with his imaginary noises. Tania felt her temper rising at the thought —and Bryden came in at that moment, and saw her face. She smouldered at him.

'Hurt?' he asked, but he knew.

She didn't answer. Now was not the time. Later, later.

He applied the ointment with a careful, gentle touch, said: 'Are you okay now?'

'Yes.'

'Then I'm going out again. I'll not be long.'

'To find your burglars?' The sarcasm dripped from her voice.

'To check up—alone.'

'Don't you want to take Ben?'

'No. I move quieter by myself.'

'Hah! You really think there's anyone there?' She couldn't keep the scorn from her face. His answering look froze her.

'I don't know—that's why I'm going. I'll not be long.'

He meant it. He really did think—she caught her breath. His face held a dark seriousness that was chilling and frightening. And she knew that she didn't want him to go. She feared for him. She was sobered now, and felt cold.

'You really mean it, don't you?'

'Yes. I'll make you a cup of tea before I go. Perhaps the longer I wait the better. I'll leave by the back. Bolt the door after me—I'll take my front door key.' He walked out. Tania couldn't stay there. She followed him, careful not to bump her arm, walking quietly, and saw him filling the kettle.

He turned. 'You're supposed to be sitting down quietly, recovering.'

'There's nothing wrong with me. My arm will be okay soon.'

He smiled. 'You must be tough. That's good. Sit down, don't stand. This won't be a minute.'

She sat down at the table and watched him. It wasn't too late. 'Look,' she said, 'just suppose there's anyone prowling round the Grange—which I doubt—have you *thought* it through? I mean, suppose there's two—or three——'

'Ah, you think there *might* be?'

'No! But if—if there *are*——' She stopped.

'You don't want me getting beaten up?' Bryden finished for her, and saw by her face that he was right. 'I am touched by your concern.' A gentle smile followed the words.

'Oh!' she sighed, exasperated. 'Serve you right if you were——'

'But I won't be. Think, Tania. If anyone was lurking before, after your dramatic departure they'll be quite sure we're safely occupied for the next few hours. You did me a good turn, actually——'

'Oh!' She stamped her foot in sheer frustration.

'And stop keep saying "oh" like that. I'm a very sneaky person. I can move quietly—that gives me the element of surprise, don't you see?'

'No, I damned well don't. Don't *you* see? How well will you do against three men?'

'Three, is it? You seem set on that. Okay, three it is. And how do you think they'll be armed? With guns?' The conversation was assuming a dreamlike quality, Tania couldn't believe it was actually happening. 'They'll just be ordinary men—if they exist—out to cause as much damage as possible in the shortest possible time——' Bryden paused to fill the teapot. 'I know how a man like Latham works. He just lost one of his good men today—he'll be scared of losing more. But he won't want anything connected with him. He'll be careful not to be involved directly—but I'm damned sure he won't just sit back and accept what's happening. A man like that doesn't like to be bested in an argument or a business deal. And, whether you believe it or not, I did hear something tonight that wasn't a normal night-time sound. I've got exceptionally keen hearing—and I heard something. There was no one in the Grange when we went or I would have heard them. So, just to satisfy myself, I'm going out, very quietly and cautiously, to check. And I can defend myself adequately against any form of attack, I promise you.'

Tania sipped her hot tea. There seemed nothing to say. There never was against him. He always had an answer. 'Be careful,' she said.

'I will. I'm going now. I've got my key.' He patted his jeans pocket. 'Lock this door. Don't wait up.' He opened the door and was gone.

Tania bolted it. He had already vanished. She looked

out of the window, but could see nothing. As silently as a shadow, Bryden had been swallowed up by the night.

Now the waiting began. She went back to the lounge and drew the curtains, was glad that Ben was with her. He padded silently along with her and sat by her side as she tried to read a magazine. It was no use at all; she couldn't even concentrate on the letters page. Her arm ached, but not intolerably so. Suppose he *was* right? She hoped he wasn't. She hoped he would return in fifteen minutes to say it had all been a false alarm, but now, reluctantly, she was forced to agree with him. Latham would not like Jim leaving him. And she had seen Latham in a temper once, when she had been at the house on an evening visit with Ted and a telephone call had come that had transformed him from a fairly genial host to a terrifying, white-faced stranger. She had felt the chill of shock then, at the sudden change caused by someone phoning to say that a contract had fallen through. She had found out afterwards, from Ted, that it had been a building contract he regarded as important and been convinced of getting.

Yes, he was capable of almost anything. Tania found that her nails were digging into her palms as she relived that memory. She was frightened now for Bryden's safety. And what could she do? If she telephoned the police there was only George Medley in the village, and how soon could he get there on his bike? It was almost frightening, the thought of how alone Bryden was. It would be all right, of course it would be. There would be no one there. Things like that didn't happen. Latham was naturally furious, but his fury would extend only to getting a solicitor's advice to see if there was any way he could get round the immovable object—namely John

Temple. Of course, she had been over-imaginative, as always, her vivid imaginings fired by Bryden, who probably wanted to frighten her——

'Huh!' she said out loud. It made her feel better, so she did it again. That was it: he was exacting a childish revenge for her behaviour. Still, she didn't feel like going to bed until he had returned. It was past eleven now, but tomorrow was Sunday and there was no need to get up early. She sat back on the settee, after switching on the television to a late night film, and prepared to wait. She wasn't going to lose her temper when he returned, but she did have a few choice words to say to him. . . .

Which was why what happened half an hour later was so utterly shocking. Tania was in an almost relaxed mood, with a good Rock Hudson/Doris Day comedy to take her mind off everything except the immediate present, when the front door was opened with a crash that almost shook the house, and she heard Bryden's voice:

'Get in! Don't argue—I'm not in the mood——'

She jumped to her feet and ran to the door to see him standing in the hall with a man who was built like a barn door, was a complete stranger, and had a very ugly expression on his face. Bryden had the man's arm twisted behind his back. He gave Tania a brief glance. 'Can I take him in the kitchen?'

She had to hold Ben's collar—he was quivering for action. Stunned, she nodded, locked Ben in the lounge, where he immediately began his desperate, excited bark, and followed them out.

The man sat on a stool and glowered at her. 'Right,' said Bryden. 'I know *who* sent you, and just before I phone him to come and collect you, I want to know why.'

The man looked up. 'I don't know what the hell you're talking about,' he muttered. 'I was only looking for rabbits——'

'Cut the fairy stories out, I'm not in the mood for those either. You were intent on doing as much damage as possible—you and your friend——' a thin smile. 'I'll know him again too. You have a choice. Either you tell me or I telephone the York police and lay charges not only against Latham but you as well. There's enough evidence of your intent up at the Grange—and hammers carry fingerprints—and it wouldn't surprise me at all if yours were already on police file. Turn out your wallet.'

'I haven't got one on——'

Bryden went over to him and lifted him to his feet. 'I'm not a patient man. Don't make me lose my temper. You saw what I did to your companion——'

The man flung a wallet from his back pocket on to the table. Tania stood riveted just inside the door, unable to move. It wasn't happening. It *couldn't* be. But it was, and it was a nightmare. She was rigid with shock.

Bryden let go of him and opened the wallet. He took out a credit card and looked at the name on it, then riffled through the rest of the contents, drew out an envelope and read that too. He handed it to Tania. 'Copy that, will you?'

She found she could move, took the envelope from him, found her notepad and copied down the man's name and address, which was on the outskirts of York.

'So if I have any more trouble, I'll know where to go, won't I?' said Bryden. 'But there won't be, I'm sure. You look a sensible man—no, don't try to move, I'd love the chance to give you a good hiding—and I've got more tough friends to call on than Jack Latham will ever have. I hope I'm making myself clear?' he added politely.

The man spoke. 'It was only a bit of a joke,' he said. 'Can't you——'

'No, I can't see that. My sense of humour is evidently different from yours. I don't appreciate men breaking into the house I'm in charge of armed with hammers and tins of paraffin——' Tania felt sick. 'And I'm getting fed up with listening to you. Now, what did Jack Latham tell you to do, and how much did he pay you?'

'He said you'd done him the dirty on a deal and he wanted you teaching a lesson but to make it look like an accident——'

'How the hell were you going to do that?'

The man shrugged. 'It's easy. He said the inside's a mess. Start a fire in an upstairs cupboard to make it look as though someone had dropped a cigarette end and it had smouldered, and once it got going to get out fast.'

'You didn't stop to think that the fire brigade can usually tell when paraffin's been used?'

He shrugged. 'That's not my problem. He said there'd be no tie-up——'

'There is now.' Bryden said it in deadly calm tones that had more effect than if he had shouted the words. 'And I suppose he'll have a dozen people who'll swear he spent this evening with them?'

'He's having a party,' the man muttered.

'Is he now? I'm just about to break it up. How much did he pay you?'

'Twenty quid before, another thirty tomorrow.'

'Well, friend, you've lost that thirty. My heart bleeds for you. I'm going to phone him. I don't advise you to move a muscle—I can see you from the hall.' He began to walk towards the door, towards Tania.

'Wait,' said the man. 'Look, he'll be mad—you've found out what you want to know. Can't you let me——'

'You should have thought of that before you decided to do his dirty work for him. Oh no, I want you here when he arrives.' Bryden walked out.

Tania felt almost sorry for the man. Bryden had left the hall door wide open. 'I'll make you a cup of tea,' she said.

'Have you got a drop of something stronger?'

She looked at him. 'I have, but I'm not wasting it on you. Be thankful you're getting tea and not a pair of handcuffs.' She wasn't frightened of him, not only because of the obvious fact that Bryden was only yards away, but because she could feel only a cold anger at what Jack Latham had tried to do. She put the kettle on. Bryden was waiting for Latham to come to the telephone; she had heard his voice asking for him.

She heard him again, moments later. 'Latham? If you want to keep out of the hands of the police I suggest you get over here right away. I've got one of your strong-arm boys and he's been talking. I'll give you fifteen minutes. If you're not here by then I'm calling York police.' He put the telephone down.

Sitting opposite the man, Bryden demanded: 'And how many times has Latham used you for his dirty work?'

'I'm saying nothing,' the man replied. Tania passed him a beaker of tea, resisting the impulse to throw it over him.

'That's all right. You will.' Bryden smiled. 'There's still fifteen minutes before he arrives. I can do a lot in that time.'

'But you wouldn't. I know my rights.'

'Oh, you mean you'd feel like reporting me to the police? I wouldn't say you're in any position to do that, chum. Have you ever had your arms broken?' he added in conversational tones.

The man looked at him, and Bryden looked back, very levelly, quite unsmiling. 'Oh yes, I mean it,' said Bryden softly. 'I want to know, *now*, exactly how often you've done this kind of nasty work for him.'

'Nothing like this, honest. But he owns apartments in York—sometimes he's wanted tenants out—and we've put the pressure on, that's all. No harm done——'

'I'm sure not. You mean old people, single people—the sort who wouldn't give much trouble? Oh yes, I see. Nice man. Nice landlord.' Bryden smiled thinly. 'I don't like bullies. I don't like *you*, Mr Taylor, particularly, and I don't like your friend. I do hope he doesn't crash his van. He wasn't in a very good state to drive when he ran towards it. Tell him what I said, won't you? I don't want to see him again. And after Monday there'll be guard dogs in the Grange—and other surprises. But most of all I don't like Jack Latham. I advise you most strongly to refuse any further commissions from him, unless, of course, they're for good honest toil.' His eyes were like ice, the startling blue cold enough to freeze.

Taylor shook his head. 'You're not getting the police?'

'Not this time. I can deal effectively with people like you, and him, myself.'

Taylor nodded. 'Was it karate?'

'You noticed? I've got a black belt in karate and akaido. I could kill you if I wanted with one blow of this hand.' He held up his right hand, fingers extended, very casually, and Tania saw the man go white. Then she knew why Taylor had come into the house so submissively and been so lacking in aggression. And she had been worried about Bryden! It seemed to have been a wasted exercise. It also made her remember something he had once said, and she felt herself go warm. Dear Lord, she wouldn't stand a chance against him if he *really* wanted to make love to her. Strangely, the feeling wasn't frightening, it was as though there were an inevitability about it.

'I can hear his car. Will you open the door, Tania?' She hadn't heard anything, and she couldn't yet. But knowing his acute hearing, she went into the hall and opened the front door to see a furious Jack Latham stepping out of his Mercedes.

He strode past her as if she didn't exist, his face flushed, his evening suit dishevelled, and went straight towards the kitchen. Tania couldn't take any more. She slipped into the lounge and sat down, hugging Ben, trying to shut her ears to the voices from the kitchen. She didn't want to hear anything any more. Her arm hurt, her head ached, she wanted to go to bed, preferably with a couple of sleeping pills, but she possessed none and had never used them. She had always slept soundly, but that was before Bryden erupted into her life. 'Oh, Ben,' she murmured. 'What shall I do? Why did I choose him to fall for?' Ben wagged his tail, as if he understood.

She heard the voices coming nearer, the door closing, then a car starting up. Bryden opened the door to the lounge. 'They've gone. Tania, I'm sorry. Truly sorry.'

'What for?' She looked up at him. 'My life has been in chaos ever since you arrived. I should b-be getting used to it by now,' and she burst into tears, stood up, and rushed past him and up the stairs, sobbing.

She was in bed lying down when she heard him tap at

her door. 'Go *away*!' she called.

'Are you respectable?'

'No,' she said. 'G-go away——'

He opened the door a fraction and peeped in, ready, it seemed, to withdraw if indeed she were not fully clothed. Then, seeing her in bed, he came in.

'I've brought you warm milk and honey,' he said, and sat on the edge of the bed. 'And two aspirins. Take them, they'll do you good.'

'No, they won't. The only thing that'll do me any good is you leaving,' she whispered. But she took the proffered beaker and the two pills and swallowed the aspirins obediently.

'Poor Tania,' he said. 'I know how you feel.'

'How c-can you?' she retorted, with some spirit. 'You spend your life g-going around karate-chopping people who get in your way——'

'Truly I'm not like that. I'm sorry, I told you. But I had to bring him here so that I could find out as much as I could before phoning.'

'You cause *chaos*, that's what you do,' she said crossly. 'And I'm not going to argue with you because you always *win*!'

'Tania, listen to me. Do you want me to leave here?' The question took her completely by surprise.

'W-where would you go?' she stammered.

'I'd sleep on a floor in the Grange. I must be here for obvious reasons. But if that is what you want, I'll go.'

He meant it too. The thought was unbearable. Yet she had just told him——.

'There's no water, no heat——'

'I know. I'll survive.' He was looking at her, and her heart ached for him.

'I couldn't,' she said quietly, suddenly subdued at the reality of what he said. 'I couldn't let you. Not yet. Not until there's water and electricity——'

'And then I'll go. I didn't want to disrupt your life like this, believe me. But then I didn't know I'd have anyone like Latham to deal with.' He shrugged. 'If he hadn't been here, none of these complications would have happened.'

'I know.' It was perhaps the first time there had been no tension in the air, which considering that she was rather vulnerable, in bed, was very surprising. Yet there was none. Bryden was being very gentle, for him, and he sat a respectable distance away, nearly at the foot of her bed, and he was being very correct. It was almost funny, but she didn't want to smile. She wanted to cry.

'I don't think he'll give any more trouble,' he said. 'He's a frightened man.'

He stood up. 'I'll go now. I'll have one last check up at the Grange, see it's locked properly—but I'll only be five minutes. Goodnight, Tania. Sleep well. I hope your arm's better in the morning.'

He smiled at her, then went out. She closed her eyes, seeing his beloved face, seeing again the slightly crooked smile he had given her just before going out, and the memory of it lingered until she drifted off to sleep a while later, after hearing him return and bolt the front door. It was the sound she had been waiting for. Then she slept.

She awoke late the next morning. The sun flooded through the window, filling the room with warm gold, and the birds trilled busily in the trees, chiding her for being late with their breakfast. Tania groaned when she tried to move her arm. It was stiff and painful, not unnaturally. She put on her dressing gown, with difficulty, and went downstairs to let Ben out.

There was no sign of Bryden. She didn't even know if he was still in bed or had gone to the Grange to work. She turned on the radio and began to prepare her breakfast, with great difficulty, working left-handed to save using her bad arm.

She had just prepared her toast and was trying to butter it when she heard Bryden's step on the stairs. He came in, saw her struggles and came over.

'Let me do that. Is your arm painful?'

'Very stiff. I thought I'd rest it. I didn't realise how difficult it was to work one-handed.'

'No drawing for you for a few days, then. See the doctor tomorrow, just to be sure.'

'I will.' She sat down and he handed her the buttered toast.

'I'll make the tea. Jim's calling later on for a talk. I'll go up to the Grange when he arrives. Have you any jobs that need doing before I go?'

'No, thanks. I'll manage anyway.'

'Sure? Would you like me to phone, see if Beth can come with him?'

She smiled. 'That sounds a good idea. She'll probably bring the girls with her. Why not? Would you?'

'Sure.' He looked at his watch. 'Nearly eleven. Think they'll be up yet?'

'Yes.'

'I'll phone now. I'll explain that you've hurt your arm.'

Tania ate her breakfast while Bryden telephoned, listening idly. Judging by his words, it seemed Beth was only too pleased to come. She gave a little sigh. Just what she needed, someone to talk to. The day began to seem a little brighter.

'All fixed. No work for you today. Beth's coming with him—and says not to worry about food, she's bringing enough for everyone and will do the cooking.' He looked at her. 'I have a couple of calls to make to London. May I?'

'Yes. If they're private, phone from the bedroom.'

'I'd prefer it, if you don't mind.' He snatched two pieces of toast from the grill in the nick of time. 'I'll eat this, make the tea, and take mine up.'

'Feel free.'

A few moments later he was on his way up. Tania heard her bedroom door close, and suddenly was struck by the feeling that these were calls of great significance. Nothing she could put her finger on. Bryden had certainly asked casually enough, yet the feeling persisted and refused to go away. She could hear the murmur of his voice from upstairs, words indistinguishable, and she knew, she just *knew*, that something was changing. What, she couldn't imagine.

When he came down his face gave nothing away. 'All done. Don't forget to let me have the telephone bill when it arrives.'

'Oh, I won't,' she assured him. 'I'd never be able to afford it!'

He laughed. He was different this morning. He seemed relaxed, and the feeling was transmitted to her. It was as if, she thought, he had decided to be charming. It was certainly working. He had a charisma all his own. It was disconcerting, Tania realised, because she was used to the tension that seemed inevitable whenever they were alone, and it caught her off balance.

'I'll take Ben for a walk if you like,' he said.

'Yes—he'd enjoy one. I'll go and get dressed. Excuse me.' She didn't understand him, and she never would, because soon he would be gone for ever. As she dressed —with difficulty—she thought about all that had happened since he'd arrived. Perhaps today would be peaceful for a change. And Beth would be here as well. She smiled to herself. She had quite a lot to tell her. Then perhaps she would be able to see everything in perspective. She put some lipstick on and went downstairs.

Late evening Sunday, and all was quiet. Bryden was out with Ben; Beth, Jim and her daughters had gone an hour or so previously, and they had all had a wonderful day, full of laughter and fun, as though Jack Latham and all problems connected with him didn't exist. Beth's two girls had taken an instant liking to Bryden, you could see that, and they had all seen another, slightly surprising facet to his character as he had done some fantastic sleight-of-hand tricks, a few of which he had afterwards taught them in order to dazzle their school friends.

'They're quite smitten,' whispered Beth, when she and Tania were alone in the kitchen, making yet another pot of tea in the early evening. 'Mind you, I can see why.' And she sighed, making Tania laugh.

Now the day was over, and it was school tomorrow. Then, on Tuesday, the holidays began. Tania straightened a cushion, looked round to see everything was off, and went up to bed.

She woke early on Monday morning because someone was knocking loudly at the front door. Groaning, Tania pulled on her dressing gown and went down, shouting at

Ben to be quiet as he added to the noise by barking.

She opened the door, still half asleep, to see a mail van outside and a smiling postman holding a registered package. ''Morning. Sign, please,' he said cheerfully, probably on the principle that if he had to be up, he didn't see why anyone should laze in bed.

Tania took the large bulky package, signed where he indicated, thanked him, and went to open it. She sat down in the kitchen after letting Ben out and putting the kettle on, yawned, and began to unravel the string and sealing wax which abounded, muttering some unladylike words under her breath as she did so.

Successful, eventually, she opened the large envelope and took out the thick bundle of papers it contained, her as yet unawakened brain still puzzled.

One second later, when she saw what lay on the table before her, she was suddenly wide awake. She was holding the deeds to the Lodge cottage in her hand. With trembling fingers she picked up the letter with them, and read it.

Then, very carefully, because she didn't believe what she had read that first time, she re-read it. There was no mistake. She was now the full and sole owner of Grange Lodge cottage. All that was necessary was her witnessed signature, and acknowledgement. She looked around her in shocked disbelief. This, her home, was all *hers*.

Bryden's voice came from behind. 'Good morning. Did I hear knocking?'

She turned. Silently she handed him the letter, which he read. Then he looked up. 'Congratulations,' he said. 'You just became a house-owner.'

'I know.' She looked at him, dazed. 'But—why? I don't understand *why*.'

CHAPTER TEN

Bryden sat down opposite her. 'It seems clear enough to me,' he said. 'The solicitor's—John Temple's, of course—and it's Philip's signature at the bottom—have evidently had instructions from John Temple to give you the deeds.'

'I think that much has sunk in already,' she said slowly. 'But I don't see why. Why *now*—when he's going to move in?'

He shrugged. 'Your guess is as good as mine. But I'll hazard one. Your grandfather served the Colonel well for many years, don't forget. Perhaps it's a belated thank you. Perhaps he doesn't feel he deserves the Lodge as well as the Grange.' He smiled. 'It's all yours anyway. *That's* clear enough.'

'I think I need a drink,' she said faintly.

'Coming up. Just sit.' Tania was not capable of doing otherwise. It changed everything. In one brief minute of time, her life had altered. The letter had said that while the Lodge was hers to do with exactly as she chose, they would appreciate her giving John Temple first chance to buy if ever she wished to sell. But now she didn't. She had security, a home of her own, something she had never envisaged in her wildest dreams.

'Here, drink this.' A beaker was placed gently at her hand.

'Thanks,' she said.

'Toast?'

'Please.' She looked up. 'Did you say he was coming on Thursday?'

'I did. You can thank him then.'

She looked down at the letter again. It's too much,' she said. 'I can't accept.'

'Can't? Or won't—due to pride?' Bryden had that half smile on his face. And he was too near the truth.

'It's not that,' she said, 'well, not exactly.' What was the use of trying to fool him? 'It's just that—well, this cottage must be worth quite a few thousand. I've done nothing to deserve it, don't you see?'

'Then why don't you talk to John Temple about it on Thursday? Tell him what you've told me. Do you think a few thousand means much to a man like him?'

'I wouldn't know.' She looked up at him. 'But it does to *me*. That's the important thing.'

'You've got strong principles, haven't you?' he commented.

'You make it sound as though that's unusual.'

'In this day and age—yes, it is.' He sat down at the table. 'It's everyone for themselves, or hadn't you noticed?'

'Is that what you're like?' she retorted.

He shook his head. 'We're not talking about me, we're talking about you.'

'But I'm asking *you* now.' Her eyes were very clear upon him, clear and honest, and she saw the answering response in his own.

'No, I don't think so,' he said, as if giving it great thought. 'I try—I have tried to live my life fairly—but I'm different from you.'

'Oh, you mean you're a man?' she said sweetly. 'Tough, independent—not fragile like little me?'

'I didn't mean that, and you know it,' he responded calmly. 'And you're not fragile by any means. You may look it, but you're far from it. You're tough like me— we're two of a kind, Tania.' He smiled.

Two of a kind! That was a laugh. But she didn't feel like laughing because she loved him and it hurt like hell.

'I'm different from you in that I've travelled,' he went on, 'I've had all the rough edges smoothed down if you like, seen the world and made my own summing up. Sometimes I haven't liked what I've seen. I've not always liked myself in the past, for that matter, and now, at the ripe old age of thirty-five, I've developed my own philosophy—my own rules, to put it another way. And I live by them.'

His words had an odd effect. For the first time Tania saw yet another facet of his complex character. She said quietly: Is that why you're working on the Grange? Doing it up in the best way you can—for someone else?'

'Yes. It's what I want to do. I'll get great satisfaction from seeing it grow, and change, and become a beautiful home again. You get a similar satisfaction from your teaching, I know that—you don't even need to tell me. Which is why I advise you to give some serious thought to keeping the Lodge. Perhaps you are needed here, more than you know.'

Tania looked down at the deeds on the table and touched the faded papers gently. 'You've made me think,' she said softly.

'And that's what I intended.' Bryden stood up. 'Toast?' The subject was closed.

'Yes. I'll make it for us.'

'No, go and get ready for school. I don't have to be out of here in half an hour—you do.'

'Heavens! Is that the time?' She looked at him in alarm. All sense of time had been lost since the post had arrived. 'I'd better dash. Yes, please, I'd like toast.' She fled upstairs to wash and dress.

She set off on time, leaving Bryden in the Lodge with Ben, and as she rode to school, her mind was full of all that had happened. Her arm still ached, but it was better now, and she looked forward to her day at school. Soon, holidays, on Wednesday a visit to York, and on Thursday she would meet for the first time the man who had given her the Lodge. He had made the gift as casually as she gave sweets to her pupils at end of term. Perhaps that was all it meant to him. Bryden had implied he was wealthy beyond anything she could imagine. His sister Margo was certainly charming enough, perhaps John Temple would be the same. She hoped so. And yet could she stay? Could she accept such a gift? Not only because of its magnitude but because there would always be the links with Bryden. Bryden the wanderer, the jack of all trades—Bryden, who might marry Margo. . . .

Nearly at school, and no more time to think, which was a relief, for she was finding her thoughts confusing. Beth would help. The sooner she had a talk with her, the better. She drove her scooter into the staff yard, was greeted by several of her class from the adjoining playground, and waved back to them. For the next seven hours she was going to put Bryden completely out of her mind. She hoped. . . .

All was quiet at the Lodge when she returned home that afternoon and made herself a cup of coffee. She sat back on the lounge settee with a sigh of relief and kicked off her shoes. 'Ah, that's better!' Soon she would go up to the Grange and see what was going on. But the next ten minutes were her own. Ben came padding in from the back garden and looked at her reproachfully. 'All right,' she said. 'I'll take you out in a few minutes——'

The telephone's shrill ring interrupted her and she got up reluctantly to answer it. 'Hello?'

'Tania? It's Margo Temple here. Is it possible to speak to my—to Bryden? It's rather urgent.'

'Oh, Margo! Well, he's up at the Grange, I think. I've only just got in from school myself. It's no use you hanging on. Shall I go and tell him and get him to call you back?'

'Please. Would you be so kind? I've been ringing all day at intervals——'

'Look, I'll go now. Can I have your number?'

'He knows it. Thanks, Tania. And thank you for the visit on Saturday. I enjoyed meeting you. Tell him I'll be waiting for his call—it's very important.'

'Yes, I will. Goodbye.' She hung up, and the flare of jealousy came as she replaced the phone so that her hand shook and she nearly dropped the receiver. She hadn't missed that intrusive 'my' at the beginning. What had Margo been going to say? 'My sweetheart' or 'my lover'? And how important was the message? Too important to be told to Tania—or too secret and private?

She put on her shoes, called Ben, and set off walking up the long drive to the Grange. The first things that struck here were the number of vans parked at front and side, and the bustle and activity.

A man was unloading rolls of wire from the nearest, and she recognised him as from the village. He greeted her cheerily.

'Hello. Is Mr Kane inside?' she called as she walked towards him.

'Yes, miss, he's upstairs with Jim. You don't recognise

me, do you? My little girl Jean is in your class.'

'Oh yes! Of course—it's Mr Armitage. I'm sorry, I was miles away.'

She went past him and up the steps to be greeted by the sounds of hammering from various parts of the house, a man's voice raised in song, and, more distantly, someone whistling.

She ran upstairs and saw Bryden first. He was deep in conversation with Jim, both men looking at plans.

'Bryden? I'm sorry to interrupt you at work, but Margo phoned and wants you to ring her back. It's very urgent.'

He looked round at her, then at Jim. 'Damn! Sorry, Jim, I'd better go. Thanks, Tania.' To Jim he added: 'I'll not be long.' He ran down the stairs. Tania couldn't go back, not yet.

Smiling brightly at Jim—it was easier to hide pain behind a smile—she said: 'Well, you certainly know how to get things going. It's like a beehive in here!'

He laughed. 'You'd be surprised how many men are fed up with working for Jack Latham! I've got more lined up if Bryden needs them.' He was dusty and dirty, his face streaked with sweat—but he looked a contented man. He folded up the plans and stuck them in his back pocket. Bryden had looked equally black, she realised now. Perhaps he intended joining in more than supervising.

'How are you getting on with Bryden?' she asked. She knew Jim well enough to ask.

'He's great. He told me that he knew nothing, and was going to rely on me—but he picks things up fast. He's more like a workmate than a boss. I'm going to enjoy this job—thanks to you, Tania.'

'Don't thank me!' she laughed. 'But what do you mean, he said he knew nothing? I thought he'd done this kind of thing before?'

Jim looked vague. 'Well, not from what I gathered. I got the impression his work's been more on paperwork lines—you know, perhaps clerical.' He shrugged. 'He's a brain for figures all right. Like a ruddy computer if you ask me. He can work out plans and figures in his head quicker than I can on paper.' He scratched his ear thoughtfully. 'He puzzles me, that man does, Tania.'

'Mmm, I know what you mean,' she murmured.

'I mean, have you seen his hands?' He held his own, heavily calloused, out, while Tania held her breath, remembering Bryden's hands very well....

'You'd think he'd never done manual work in his life. Look at mine. But he's swung into action as if he was born to it. Strong as a horse, and never gets tired—but, I dunno, there's *something*'—he frowned, 'I can't put my finger on it'—he lowered his voice as a man passed, bearing planks over his shoulder, 'it's like a game to him.'

'A game?' She looked round. Perhaps it was. Maybe he was doing it all for Margo, to prove his love for her. 'It looks like hard work from where I'm standing. Did he tell you about Latham's men?'

'Just said there'd been a bit of trouble, and it had been sorted out. There's a guard dog coming every night from a security firm in York until we can get the electricity fixed, so I gather Latham has tried to cause trouble.'

'That's putting it mildly! I hope he doesn't try it with you.'

'He won't, because he knows damned well if he does I'll go round to his mansion and punch him on the nose.' Tania smiled. He would too.

'I'd better go back and get some work done,' she said. 'I'm supposed to be drawing the rooms as they were— but I suppose I'll have to do it at weekends and evenings now it's all happening. I'll see you, Jim.'

'See you, Tania.' As she ran down the stairs she looked back. He was already engrossed in the plans again.

Bryden was still on the telephone as she opened the front door of the Lodge, and she hesitated, indecisive. Did she go in—or wait? If she waited he might think she was listening. She pushed open the door. It was her telephone—and surely he'd have said all the secret bits by now? Like telling her how much he loved her....

'Okay. 'Bye.' He replaced the telephone and looked at her. 'Thanks, Tania. Sorry I had to drag you up there, but it was quite important. Any chance of a cup of tea while I'm here?'

'Help yourself. The kettle should still be hot. I was about to have a cup when the phone rang.' She couldn't keep the coolness out of her voice. She tried, but it came out like that and she decided she didn't care anyway. Damn him. And damn Margo.

'I'll make you one as well.' He walked away as if he hadn't been aware of the slight formation of icicles and she heard the gas go on. She took out her half empty beaker and rinsed it, and looked at his hands. Bryden caught her look and said: 'I'd better wash these.'

She sat down. 'I shouldn't bother. You'll only get them dirty again.'

'Never mind.' He whistled as he washed them, then held them out for inspection. 'Okay?'

'I suppose so.' She looked more closely. 'My, you've got blisters! Oh dear, you'd better put plasters on.' She stood up and went for her first aid box, while he filled the teapot. 'Sit down,' she said, and began cutting strips of adhesive tape. 'Dear me, you'd better watch those. You *have* been working hard, haven't you?'

He looked up at her, and that look stopped her in her tracks. 'All right,' he said softly, 'get to the point. You're enjoying this, aren't you?'

And the tension grew imperceptibly from nothing to a shimmering vibration in seconds, so that she caught her breath, and was afraid. For a moment she couldn't answer.

'Well?' he said.

'You've not done this kind of work before, have you?' she managed.

'Because of a few blisters? You get those if you start gardening after winter——'

She took his left hand and held it palm uppermost. It was a very strong hand, hard, big—but the telltale blisters at the base of the fingers told their story clearly. And as she looked, as she was about to say, he closed his fingers over hers and held them so tightly that she couldn't move. The tension was quite unbearable, and she wanted to get away. . . .

'Now, what were you saying?' he demanded.

'You're hurting me, Bryden——'

'Good. I'll go on hurting you until you tell me the meaning behind your snide little cracks.' He increased the pressure, making her wince.

'All right,' she gasped. 'Let me *go*! I'll tell you——'

He released her so suddenly that her hand felt weightless for a second. Before she could think what she was doing, she caught him a resounding slap on his face, taking him completely by surprise. 'Don't ever do that again!' she snapped—then, backing, as he stood up, 'No—don't——'

He stopped, smiled slowly, dangerously, the mark she

had left on his cheek fast fading. 'Temper,' he said softly. 'By God, you've a temper on you, lady——'

She turned, to run, and he caught her and whirled her round and held her arms and looked at her, and his eyes were hard but he didn't seem to be angry, he seemed to be enjoying himself. Ben whined softly and Bryden looked down at him: 'It's all right, I'm not going to hurt her, Ben—just teach her a lesson.'

'You're not! Just let me go at——'

'When I've finished, pretty lady. Is it rough men you prefer? I can be rough.'

'I know you can,' she gasped. 'Look, I'm sorry I hit you. Is that what you want to hear?—but you annoyed me, squeezing my hand——'

'And I said I wanted to know why all the cracks——'

'All *right*, I'll tell you. I think you're a phoney! I don't think you've ever worked like that before. I think—I think——' she stopped.

'Yes?'

'I don't know! Let me go, please.'

For answer he put his arms round her, held her tightly, and kissed her. His kiss was hard, and had a salty taste, and he was being rough, and he hadn't shaved, which chafed her skin, but if he knew, he didn't care, and when he released her she was weak and breathless—and he knew. He laughed softly, and took hold of her again, and this time, when he kissed her, it was very different. He kissed her gently, his lips tender, his hands and body hard, and that was right too. Tania responded, the love within her flooding out to surround him, filling her senses with the heady delight in which nothing else mattered. 'Oh, my God,' he murmured, and put up now gentle hands to lay on her cheeks, so that he held her tenderly and kissed her again, his mouth searching hers.

Then, slowly, inexorably, he released her, and looked down at her, eyes dark with passion and a deep excitement that sent a shiver through her. He put his hand to her throat where the pulse beat, and his thumb was lightly on it, and he asked: 'Why does your heart beat so fast?'

'B-because you frighten me,' she whispered.

'Oh, no, that wasn't fear.' He moved his hand slightly, to tilt her chin up. 'Look into my eyes and tell me I frighten you again.' His voice was a husky, throaty murmur. She couldn't move away, although she was free to do so, but she didn't want to, and he knew it. The tension had changed to a soft wave that wrapped round them both like a cloak, sheltering them, and both were equally aware of it, and there was a kind of magic in the room that reached out to touch them. Tania wanted to tell him the words she held within her—I love you—but she could not, must not, for that was her secret, and he would never know.

'You do sometimes,' she whispered, and he slid his hands gently round her, and there was nothing frightening there, there was only safety and a great calm and peace; it filled her very being so that she closed her eyes, and Bryden pulled her towards him so that she was pressed against his chest.

'Oh, Tania.' He had bent his head, so that the words were a quiet murmur in her ear. 'You know what's inevitable now, don't you? You know that one day we'll make love—not yet, the time is not yet, but it will happen——' She didn't want to hear, she didn't want him to say the words, she knew she shouldn't want him to—yet she stayed there, and those strong hands caressed her back, and his touch was gentle and it was right, but his words weren't, because—because there was Margo——

She murmured something, a wordless protest, but that was all. 'One day,' he repeated. 'No use to fight it. It will happen as surely as spring follows winter—but not now, not yet. We want each other, we always have——'

'No,' she whispered.

'Oh yes. Don't try to deny it. Don't you think I know? Poor Tania——' he began to laugh softly, and she heard the laughter deep in his chest and it was a gentle sound, a sharing sound, and she thought she might die because she knew the inevitability of it all now, as well as he. She lifted her face to him so that he saw the tears glistening in her eyes and the laughter died away, and he kissed her eyes, kissed the tears away, then put his fingers in her hair. 'Mmm, beautiful hair,' he murmured. 'Beautiful rich auburn tresses——'

She felt as if she might float away if he were not holding her. He was already making love to her, with soft words, with a gentle touch of fire, with his eyes, with his whole being, and nothing had ever been like this before in the world, and nothing could ever be like this again, and the memory of it would last all her life, for ever, and ever....

What would it matter that he didn't love her? What did anything matter any more? She put up her hands to him, to touch his beloved face, and kissed him. Then she smiled, and saw her smile reflected in his eyes, and the moments they had shared were drawing to a close, and that was right and inevitable too, because there would be more, she knew that now. She would question her conscience later.

'You must go back,' she said.

'Yes.' He looked at the plasters on the table. 'I'll leave those until later.' He touched her cheek. 'I won't be long.'

She watched him go, and it wasn't until he had gone that she realised the tea was now cold in the pot. He hadn't had the cup after all. She sat down in a daze, and she couldn't think about anything clearly any more. The devastating effect Bryden had had on her still lingered like some sweet perfume in the room and no coherent thoughts would come.

After what might have been only minutes, or hours, or days, she began to prepare the tea. She was scarcely aware of what she was doing.

She ate alone. And at seven, when she had heard all the vehicles pass the Lodge, and all was quiet, she went to find Bryden. The Grange had an empty look, both doors closed, and his van had gone as well. Tania knocked on the door and shouted, but there was no reply. Her first thought, that he had gone to meet Margo somewhere, was quickly dispelled by common sense. He couldn't go anywhere dressed in the clothes he wore, and in the state he was in. So where was he? She felt uneasy, unsure of herself, as she walked back with Ben. Even as she opened the front door the telephone was ringing and she dashed in and picked it up.

'Hello?'

It was Bryden. First came the pips, the sound of a coin, then his voice. 'Tania? It's me, Bryden.'

'I've just been up to look for you!' she gasped.

'I'm sorry. That's why I phoned. I left with Jim, to go and see some antiques he knew of in the village that a woman wanted to sell. Then he insisted on me going back to his house—and now we're in some quaint pub called the Wagon and Horses——'

'I know it,' she said.

'I'm setting off any time. We've just had a drink to celebrate the first day of work on the Grange—you know how it is.'

He didn't owe her any explanations. Why should he? He was a free man.

'Of course. I'll expect you when I see you.'

'I won't be long. Oh—Beth says to give her a ring, will you? She wants to fix up an evening out for the four of us. I said I'd leave it to you—anything suits me. Okay, I'll see you soon.'

'I'll call her now. 'Bye.'

''Bye.' The phone clicked, went dead, followed by the dialling tone. Tania began to dial Beth's number. It was as good a time as any to tell her about the gift of the Lodge—if Bryden had not done so already. An evening out, for the four of them. He said it so casually, as if it were entirely natural that something like that should be planned. And why not? They all got on well.

'Beth? It's me——'

'Oh, Tania love, I was just about to ring you! Bryden phoned, did he?'

'Yes. They're in a pub now.'

'I know. He says he'd like to take us out to dinner. You know me, I never say no! What about Friday?'

'Suits me. Did he tell you about my letter this morning?'

'No. What letter?' So he hadn't. Perhaps he had forgotten. Tania told her, and Beth was stunned with surprise.

'That's *marvellous*! Oh, Tania, how *super*! John Temple must be a very nice man.'

'I suppose so. I'll know on Thursday. I'm still not sure about accepting——'

'Don't be so daft!' Beth interrupted, with true Yorkshire bluntness. 'You want your head felt if you don't accept! Don't you *dare*!'

Tania laughed. 'I'll see. I'm very tempted. Look, I'll pop in to see you tomorrow. We'll talk then, and fix up about Friday.' They talked for a few minutes more, exchanging local news and gossip, and Tania heard Bryden's van, and finished the call. She felt apprehension building up and went quickly into the kitchen to get **his** tea from the oven. The memory of the scene flooded irresistibly back to her and she felt as nervous of seeing him as a young girl on her first date.

She heard the door open, Ben's noisy greeting, and called out: 'It's ready, in the kitchen.'

'Right.' He came in, big, dark, attractive, much cleaner than when she had last seen him—he'd probably had a wash at Beth and Jim's—and sat down at the table. 'This looks good,' he said. 'I'm starving. These village pubs are a revelation, aren't they? All the workmen congregate before going home, and it's a very down-to-earth atmosphere. I met a few of Jim's friends—some useful contacts there, actually. I'm glad I went.'

'And the antiques? Any good?'

He frowned. 'Nothing I fancied. I'd like you to see them, though. Perhaps you can call in with Beth some time. If there's anything you think would fit in at the Grange, get it. You know better than I.'

Tania paused as she put the kettle on. What was there in his words that had puzzled her so? She couldn't put a finger on it—yet. But there was certainly something that didn't seem to fit in.

He ate his steak and kidney pie, followed it with fresh fruit salad, and sat back, replete. 'I enjoyed that. Tania, how would you like to go out for a drink with me this evening?'

'I'd love to,' she answered promptly. 'Now?'

'No. Give me time to wash and change. The security man should be here at about eight. I'll give him a key to take the dog in, then we can leave. Don't go near the Grange at night—or in it—will you?'

'I wouldn't dare. Is that it? Do they just leave a dog there all night?'

'Yes. And collect it at eight next morning. I've arranged for it until we get properly fixed up with alarms. And by law he has to fix signs up where any intending burglars can see and be warned. So that should take half an hour, no more. We'll go about eight-thirty.'

'I'll be ready. Go and have your wash first. There's plenty of hot water. I'll clear up here.'

It was as though the interlude—that magic time—had never happened. Which was probably just as well, she thought, as she washed the plates. You couldn't balance on a high wire all the time. But she wondered if Bryden remembered as well as she did.

They went to a quiet country pub several miles away from home, and there spent a pleasant evening, with no tension, no awkwardness. Bryden was charming company, entertaining, good to be with. He drank little save white wine, and they had a supper of scampi in the basket and set off home at just past ten. He parked the van outside the Lodge and opened the front door with his key, and they went into the dark hall. Ben barked from the kitchen, and Bryden put out his hand and stopped

Tania from putting on the light. 'Wait,' he said. That was all. He closed the door, and then she was in his arms, in the darkness, as she had known she would be, all evening.

His lips searched, and found, and she revelled in the touch of him, the fire of him, and the strength, and all that he was doing to her. She held him closely to her, and the world was safe again as it would be every time she was in his arms, and she heard his breathing change, become more rapid, heard how his voice had become husky as he murmured such words she had never heard before, and they were all part of the dream, because it must be a dream, it was too wonderful to be real, and too precious to even waste a moment of it in thought. Then there was no time for that anyway because all was sensation, touch, and kiss, and emotions too deep to name, nameless, formless—bliss.

Bryden picked her up in his arms and carried her up the stairs and into her bedroom, then laid her on the bed, and she looked up at him as he towered over her, caught in the moonlight from the window, the rest—darkness. Then he moved, and that light was blotted out as he lay beside her, their bodies touching, on fire, then his hands, so gently and carefully, undoing the buttons of her blouse so that she waited, wanting to cry out, wanting to help him, but waiting, trembling, as the silky material was peeled off slowly and caressingly. Every move he made was a caress, every small touch a kind of lovemaking, and he knew, and she knew, that there would be no more waiting in a few minutes. In some small part of her mind was the knowledge that she mustn't—but her heart was saying otherwise, as was her trembling, treacherous body and mouth, and she cried out, a small sound, but he drowned it with his sweet lips and with his hands which stroked and teased her slender body. Now, soon, so very soon, she would know . . .

The telephone rang, shattering the silence with its insistent shrillness, and Bryden muttered something and lifted himself slightly away and looked at her, and she could feel his excitement, the pulsing excitement that coursed through her own veins, and telephones didn't matter. What did they matter? She pulled him to her, laughing secretly, and bit his ear and whispered:

'It'll stop——' She felt his trembling, and knew that he wanted her more than anything in life, and the knowledge was heady, an excitement in itself. The hard lean length of him was against her, his hunger unabated—but the telephone continued its shrilling interruption and he groaned and said:

'It's no use, Tania—it's going to go on for ever.' He sat up, leaving his hand at her waist, just resting there as if it belonged, and picked up the telephone.

'Hello.' His voice was so husky it was barely a whisper. And Tania waited patiently and heard: 'Can I ring you back?' and smiled to herself in the dark.

Then the magic was shattered into a million fragments —because she had heard who was on the line, and she pushed his hand away from her. Because it was Margo, and no, she wasn't going to let him ring back. She needed to speak to him now.

CHAPTER ELEVEN

BRYDEN stood up, and he was different, sober, no longer the man who had been about to make love to her, but a stranger. Talking to his mistress. 'All right,' he said. 'Tell me.' He listened. Tania went out of the room, fastening her blouse, and down the stairs. 'Come on, Ben—in the garden,' she called, and he looked at her reproachfully, but she didn't want to take him out. She wanted to go to bed—alone.

When she heard the telephone ring in the hall as it was replaced in the bedroom, she called Ben in. When Bryden came down she looked at him. 'I'm going to bed,' she said. 'Goodnight.' She brushed past him and he didn't attempt to stop her, but he said:

'Margo is like a sister to me, no more. What she had to say was very important. She'd been trying to reach me all evening.'

'And now she has.' She turned, in the doorway, trying to hide the hurt, the deep pain in her eyes. 'I'm glad she called when she did. It made me remember who I was.' Her mouth trembled. 'You must think I'm stupid, Bryden. But I won't be again.' She walked steadily out, and away from him. And when she was in her bedroom, she wedged the door with a chair.

When she awoke next morning he had gone. She left the door open for Ben, padlocked the back garden gate in the fence, and set off on her scooter for Beth's house. She had to tell someone, and she trusted Beth implicitly.

It didn't matter that the café would be busy. If necessary Tania would help. She had done so before, and enjoyed it. She just desperately needed someone to confide her muddled thoughts to—and Beth would understand—and listen.

It was busy with the morning shoppers for their elevenses, their morning coffee and cakes, but Beth said: 'It'll be over in half an hour, then we'll nip upstairs and put our feet up for ten minutes. Tony and the girls will cope.'

'It'll need more than ten minutes,' said Tania, with a rueful smile, passing her a tray of coffee cups and saucers. 'But I'll go mad if I don't tell someone——'

'I know,' Beth soothed. 'You look as though you've had a rough night. Your Aunty Beth will sort everything out.'

How nice if she could! Some problems couldn't be resolved so easily, but at least she would be able to see things in perspective. That would be something.

Half an hour later they sat in the comfortable flat above the café sipping hot coffee, and Beth said: 'Right. Out with it.'

'I'm making a fool of myself over Bryden,' sighed Tania. 'That's putting it at its simplest——'

'Look, love, don't tell me anything you'll regret,' Beth cautioned.

'I can tell you anything, and I have to talk to someone or I'll go mad. I can't get him out of my mind—ever—and last night we—went out for a drink, and afterwards——' she paused, swallowed—'we——'

'Oh God!' Beth groaned. 'Don't! You——'

'We nearly made love—oh, very nearly—only I was saved by the bell, as you might say.' Tania choked on a laugh that was nearly a sob at her own feeble attempt at humour. 'The—telephone rang and it was Margo with something urgent. I walked out and left him. Oh, Beth, I nearly made such a fool of myself! I wanted him——' She looked in anguish at her friend, wondering if there would be shock, or disgust, on her face. There was nothing save a warm concern. 'I've never wanted anyone—any man—before.'

'You're twenty-four,' Beth said wisely. 'It would be strange if you didn't. And you've met a man who has more than his share of sex-appeal, let's face it. And he's staying in your house. Good grief, you'd have to be a saint to ignore all those facts! I thought there'd be trouble when I met him—I didn't realise exactly what the complications would be——' She stopped, as if she had said something she shouldn't, and Tania looked at her, puzzled by something in her voice.

'What do you mean?'

'Oh, nothing. I meant—well, living under the same roof—you know——' she was floundering, which wasn't like Beth at all, and Tania stood up.

'What's happening? What is it, Beth? What have I said? Have I—shocked you?'

'Heavens, no!' Beth laughed, and to Tania's keen ears it sounded as though in relief. 'Sit down again. More coffee?'

'Um—just a drop. What is it?'

Beth shrugged. 'Just—you know, I appreciate how difficult things must be. I don't know what to suggest either. Has it ever occurred to you that he might have fallen for you?'

'With Margo around?' Tania laughed. 'You must be joking!'

'How did he behave with her on Saturday? Did they seem madly in love?'

'No—but don't forget she's terribly upper class. I shouldn't imagine she'd show her feelings. She was just very charming.'

'But Bryden?'

Tania looked at her. 'I don't know. They knew one another very well.'

Beth gave a small, secret smile. 'That doesn't mean they're lovers.'

'Whose side are you on?' demanded Tania.

'Yours, love! I'm trying to make you *see*. It's what you came for, remember?'

'Yes. Sorry, Beth.' Tania sat down again. 'They were laughing, I remember that. Laughing like only people who know each other very well can do—and I felt a pang of sheer blinding jealousy. I hated them both at that moment.'

'They were laughing—so? Lots of people laugh when they're together—isn't it better than fighting?'

'He said—after that phone call last night, when she'd insisted on speaking to him—that she was like a sister to him. It was as if he knew how it had hurt me. But it was too late then. I left him.'

'Oh God!' Beth's laughter was a shocking intrusion, and Tania gaped at her. 'Sorry, Tania, but don't you *see*? Oh dear, girl, don't you *see*?'

'No, I don't. Now you're not making sense, Beth. I'm sorry, I mut be out of sorts today. I'd better go—you'll be busy——'

'Wait,' said Beth. 'I'm not laughing at you—oh Tania, what I meant was—they *are* brother and sister.'

The blood drained from Tania's face. 'How—how——' she began, and couldn't continue.

'Look, I'd better tell you. I wasn't going to, not till I'd found out for sure. But things have gone too far now, in more ways than one. I'm going to show you something, and then, before you go, I'm going to tell you one or two things—then *you* can do your own detective work.' She paused in the act of searching in her sideboard, and turned to Tania. 'Brace yourself. You're in for a bit of a shock, love. I put it away safely, now where did I—ah! here we are.' She stood up, and she was holding an ancient copy of the *Tatler and Bystander*. 'I was chucking out a load of old books and magazines a week or so ago, and you know me, I can't resist leafing through. When I met your Bryden I came home, rescued this one from the dustbin, and saved it. I was biding my time to tell you —and Jim, because I wanted to be sure first because it puzzled me——'

'For heaven's sake, what?' Tania gasped.

Beth opened the magazine and handed it to Tania. 'Look,' she said. 'Just look.'

There was an article on the page—and there was a photograph of several people, guests at a society wedding. Margo on the left, two men, then Bryden, and another, older woman. Dazed, Tania read 'From left: Miss Margo Temple-Kane, Mr Cassian Stevens, The Hon. Jeremy Baylis, Mr Bryden Temple-Kane and Miss Charmian Stevens at the wedding of——' She didn't read any further. She looked up at Beth, stunned.

'I don't understand,' she whispered.

'I do. Your Bryden Kane is really John Temple—he's the *owner* of the Grange, and for reasons best known to himself he's pretending to be *working* for the owner. I've not sorted that one out yet. But I must admit I'm very curious indeed.'

'But——' Bewildered, Tania looked from the photograph to Beth, 'John Temple is coming here on Thursday. How can——'

'Ever heard of a substitute? I mean, he's gone this far. I don't imagine a little thing like that would worry him.'

'Oh, I feel sick.' Tania clutched her stomach. 'Why? Why?'

'I just don't know. Would you like me to tackle him?'

'No, I'll do it. May I take this?'

'If you're sure——'

'I'm sure.' Tania's face was pale. 'But, Beth, Jim's working for him—he's left Latham——'

'That's why I kept quiet, love. But I think, oddly enough, that everything's straightforward in that direction. Jim certainly thinks so, and he's a shrewd judge of character—I just don't understand why the pretence.'

'Nor do I, but I'm going to.' Tania stood up. 'I'm going home now. I came here to try and get my poor muddled brain straightened, instead of which I'm going back more confused than ever.' She hugged Beth. 'Wish me luck.' She drew back. 'The Lodge! Beth, he gave me the Lodge!'

'Yes, I know.' Beth's eyes were very wise. 'I wonder why?'

'Tell me, why are you looking like that?' Tania's heart pounded.

'No reason. Off you go. Good luck—let me know how you go on.'

'I will.' She folded the magazine and put it in her bag. 'Goodbye, Beth.'

She was scarcely aware of the ride home. Fortunately there was little traffic on the road to the Lodge. An Electricity Board van passed her, and she could guess where that was going, but she didn't care. Bryden Kane —John Temple—the words twisted and turned in her mind. One man, two names—but why? Why? Then gradually, as she neared home, little things began to fall into place. Small facts she had ignored because they didn't fit suddenly assumed a meaning.

Bryden's comments on the village pub, ordinary enough—but as though he had never been in one before, and perhaps, if he was so wealthy, he wouldn't have. His clothes. When she had first encountered him he had been as roughly dressed as any tramp, and still was, for work, but his other clothes—particularly the sports jacket and slacks he had worn the previous evening—had been of a superb cut and cloth, yet nothing noticeable. Understated, casual, and Tania was no expert on men's clothing, but with her new awareness she suddenly knew they were extremely expensive. His hand, with the blisters from doing unaccustomed work. And the question again was—why?

She went into her house, which was empty save for Ben. Feeling almost ashamed of herself, she ran upstairs and stood inside the doorway to his bedroom. Because it was so small some clothes were on hangers on the hook on the door. She touched the jacket, and then, feeling almost as though she were stealing, she opened the jacket and looked for the label. It was small, neatly tucked away—and it was from a tailor in Miami, Florida. She let it fall back and looked round the room. Bryden kept it neat. His suitcases were under the bed, she had noticed them when he arrived, and they had puzzled her momentarily. They were of heavy hide, battered, but beautifully made. She had seen enough. To have searched his chest of drawers would have been abhorrent to her. She turned and went downstairs.

And now what did she do? Wait? She couldn't. There was only one thing for it—work. Tania put on her flowered nylon overall, covered her hair with a green headsquare, set out all the cleaning materials, and set to to clean the house. Work was the finest antidote for her. It enabled her not to have to think, or plan what she was going to say to him, because some things were so bizarre that no provision could be made. A poor man pretending to be a rich one, that she could understand. It happened all the time in varying degrees. But the other way round? Too ridiculous for words. And in a sense Bryden hadn't been dishonest. The house was his, he could employ whom he liked to work there—and he was working there himself. She scrubbed away at the kitchen paintwork vigorously, trying not to think about the questions that kept recurring. Trying to be normal. . . .

'Hello!' He had come in so silently that she jumped. 'Sorry,' he said. 'Did I startle you?'

Tania turned and faced him, well aware she must look a sight, and blurted out, before she had time to think: 'Hello, Mr *Temple-Kane*.'

She expected him to be shattered. She didn't expect the reaction she got.

'Ah.' He sat down. 'So you know, do you?'

'Is that all you've got to say?'

'For the moment—yes. When did you find out?'

She flung the magazine at him. 'This morning. At Beth's.'

He looked at the picture, nodded, then put it down. 'I see. Clever Beth.'

'Damn you!' she glared at him. 'What the hell does it all mean? Does it give you a kick, pretending to be a *peasant*?'

He started to smile. 'No. But it wasn't for that reason that I did it.'

'What, then?' She stood by the window, arms akimbo,

the light of battle in her eyes, cheeks as fiery as her hair, and he stood up slowly and walked towards her.

'I did it for you,' he said.

The words stopped her in her tracks, completely stunned her—as he had clearly expected, for he tilted her chin up and looked into her eyes, and smiled again, his crooked, wonderful, bone-melting smile, and said:

'Lost your tongue?'

'For me?' she echoed in a little whisper. 'I—don't—don't understand.'

'I'm damned sure you don't, but it was worth it just to see you speechless for once in your life. Sit down, and I'll tell you.'

'No, I'll stand.' She had to brace her legs, for they had begun to tremble, because something odd was happening to her, as though she *knew*—she knew what was about to come, and she wasn't sure if she was ready yet to hear it.

'Very well, so will I. It's quite a story. It'll take some time.'

'I'm listening,' she said, and looked at him again, saw what was in his eyes and felt warmth fill her, and added: 'I'll sit down.'

'Very wise.' He sat opposite her at the table, never taking his eyes from her. The warmth filled the room, making her breathless, making her heart beat more rapidly so that she felt almost dizzy. He spoke, softly: 'Once upon a time there was a very wealthy young man, who had been born with a golden spoon in his mouth, and who led the kind of life that most people only dream of, or see in films. He was not only very rich, he was also spoilt, because he could have anything he wanted—anything that money can buy. He jetted round the world to parties, and thought nothing of flying to Paris for dinner at Maxim's and back again the same evening to play roulette at a very exclusive London club and then perhaps, the next day, if he'd sobered up, fly to Austria for a bit of skiing—and always accompanied by beautiful ladies, you understand, who fell for him everywhere he went, and he loved it, he really did. The world was his oyster and he enjoyed it to the full, and he enjoyed the company of all those gorgeous girls—and life was quite wonderful for him.' He paused.

'You're with me so far?' he asked politely. She nodded.

'Good. Until, one day, when he was nearly thirty, the rich life began to pall. He'd done everything, been everywhere, could buy what he wanted, when he wanted it —and he woke up one day and thought about his life, and he felt repelled by himself. So he went off on an adventure trail down the Amazon, and came back feeling a little better, having seen another kind of life. Then his wealthy grandfather died, and this young man went— reluctantly—to the funeral because he didn't really care about the old fellow, but it seemed the polite thing to do —and while the funeral service was on and he stood by the graveside wondering how soon he could decently get away, he saw something that, in a sense, changed his life irrevocably. Do you want to know what he saw?'

Tania nodded, because she couldn't speak. 'He saw, on the outskirts of the throng of mourners, a red-haired girl of about eighteen or nineteen, standing by an old man. The girl was clearly upset. The tears ran down her cheeks, and she was supporting the old man by the arm, and she looked, despite her tears and sadness, incredibly beautiful, calm and serene—untouched by the world. So the spoilt young man asked someone who she was, and was told that she lived in a small cottage on the estate of his grand-father, with her grandfather. But they didn't return to the big house afterwards with the rest of the funeral party, they'd vanished when next he looked.'

He stopped. He smiled slightly at Tania. 'He couldn't get that face out of his mind. When he left for London, he took the memory with him, and he thought of all the gorgeous girls he knew who said they thought he was the most wonderful, handsome creature they'd ever seen, and he began to wonder if they would still think the same if he was poor, only he could never get the chance to find out, because of course everyone knew he'd got millions.

'Time passed, and he went to all the right places and parties and life continued its merry way—only some-thing had changed. In one part of his mind was the image he carried with him of that girl he had seen so briefly but knew now that he would never forget as long as he lived. And his grandfather had left him his old house—the young man already had three, so one more didn't make a great deal of difference to him. In fact nothing made a great deal of difference any more. So he decided to come down to his house—and see again the girl he couldn't get out of his mind, just to see if she was really as beautiful as he'd remembered.

'Then he thought about it, and he thought: What if I fall in love with her? He'd never been in love, you see. He'd had affairs, but no love. Then he thought—and what if she falls for me? And he knew he would never know, because he never had before, whether she'd fallen for his money—or him. So he decided to come down as an ordinary man, working for someone else, and see what happened. You see, he'd already found that he loved this girl—even though he wasn't prepared to admit it to himself, because it made him vulnerable, and he'd never been vulnerable in his life. He got to the house, and he met the girl, and she was exactly as he'd remembered, even more lovely. She had a fiery temper to match her hair, and wasn't afraid of socking it to him—and no one had ever done that before, so it was quite a novelty— but more. He discovered—or thought he did—that she was beginning to like him. Not as a wealthy man, but for himself.' He stopped. Tania looked at him.

'Only she found out who he was a little too soon,' she said.

He nodded. 'You *know* this fairy story?'

She shook her head, not sure whether she wanted to laugh or cry. 'Oh, Bryden, oh dear! I don't know what to say.'

'Then don't. I haven't quite finished the story. I just want to add that he—I—have found more joy in these last few days than I have in all my thirty-five years. I don't know whether that means anything to you, but it means a great deal to me.'

She couldn't speak. Tears welled up, and he came round to her and lifted her to her feet and took her in his arms. 'Please put me out of my misery,' he begged.

'I love you—is that what you want to hear? Didn't you *know*?' she whispered.

'I thought I did—oh yes, I thought I did, but to hear you say it is all I'll ever need.'

'I was jealous of Margo,' she confessed, voice muffled.

'Oh God!' he began to laugh. 'I guessed so. Trust her to come here! I'd told her, and she thinks I'm mad— but we get on fine, for brother and sister. She likes you.'

'I like her—now,' Tania admitted. 'But Thursday—who was coming?'

'A friend. A nice, anonymous friend who's madly in love with Margo—that was the reason for the panic phone calls, because he broke his leg skiing on Saturday and we were deciding what to do.' He sighed. 'Oh Tania, Tania my love, will you marry me and live at the Grange with me? Can you bear it, knowing I'm filthy rich?'

'I could learn to adjust,' she murmured, 'I suppose.'

'You'll have to try. Unless we give most of it away. And I'm tempted.'

'We'll talk that over later.' She laughed. 'I look a sight! And I was so mad with you because I couldn't understand why you'd done it—that's what puzzled me terribly. Why? Now I know——'

'Yes, now you know. That's all that matters. Go and get changed. We're going to York to buy an engagement ring.' He slapped her bottom lightly. 'Go on, off you go.'

Her eyes sparkled. 'Don't be bossy! I might not want one anyway!'

'That's my girl!' He hugged her. 'We'll argue about it on the way—okay?'

'Okay, but don't think I'll become a submissive female once we're married——'

'Heaven forbid!'

'Just so long as you understand. I'll go and change,' she said demurely, and kissed him lightly, patted his cheek, and skipped out of the kitchen, and up the stairs.

She heard his laughter following her—then she heard him walk into the hall, and the 'ting' as he removed the telephone receiver. Then she heard his footsteps on the stairs. She smiled a little smile to herself. And she waited at the top of the stairs for him.

What readers say about Harlequin Romances

"I just want you to know that I enjoy Harlequin Romances more than any book I have ever read except the Bible."
L.V.,* Rossville, Georgia

"I can think of no better way of relaxing than with a Harlequin. They allow me to face my world with a smile and new confidence."
L.F., Ames, Iowa

"Your books...are just what the doctor ordered."
K.B., Decatur, Georgia

"I get hours of relaxation and enjoyment reading Harlequins."
M.M., Middletown, New York

*Names available on request

4 FREE

Harlequin Romances

Get all the latest books before they're sold

As a Harlequin subscriber you actually receive your person
copies of the latest Romances immediately after they come
the press, so you're sure of getting all 6 each month.

Cancel your subscription whenever you wish

You don't have to buy any minimum number of books.
Whenever you decide to stop your subscription just let us kn
and we'll cancel all further shipments.

Your FREE gift includes
- *Anne Hampson* — Beyond the Sweet Waters
- *Anne Mather* — The Arrogant Duke
- *Violet Winspear* — Cap Flamingo
- *Nerina Hilliard* — Teachers Must Learn